THE FACE OF A HERO

Ayree, the Warlock, shook his head. "You do not understand all of magic yet, my sister. The world is older than magic, but not so old as prophecy."

"Prophecy!" The maiden laughed. "Are you dwelling on that foolish scroll again? Let the scroll stay lost if it worries you so."

"You will come to remember those words," said Ayree, "perhaps with regret. If the scroll falls into evil hands, we are lost. It must be found and returned by a hero."

Ayree's sister laughed again. "Well, that homeless wanderer who came here with his dog didn't look like a hero to me. He knows nothing of quests and grand deeds, that Mustapha."

Ayree said nothing, turning his eyes to the vanishing dot that was Mustapha and his wise dog riding together on the silver steed into the south land. Truly his sister was still very young, he thought, to know so little of heroes.

Worlds of Fantasy from
Avon Books

Esther M. Friesner
Mustapha and his Wise Dog

AVON
PUBLISHERS OF BARD, CAMELOT, DISCUS AND FLARE BOOKS

AVON BOOKS
A division of
The Hearst Corporation
1790 Broadway
New York, New York 10019

Copyright © 1985 by Esther M. Friesner
Published by arrangement with the author
Library of Congress Catalog Card Number: 84-91773
ISBN: 0-380-89676-1

First Avon Printing, July 1985

AVON TRADEMARK REG. U. S. PAT. OFF. AND IN
OTHER COUNTRIES, MARCA REGISTRADA, HECHO EN
U. S. A.

Printed in the U. S. A.

WFH   10   9   8   7   6   5   4   3   2   1

For my husband, W. J., the Bear who believed

Chapter I

PROLOGUE

"Vair is a land of merchants and nothing is so dear to the heart of a merchant as a trade bazaar!"

The speaker spread his plump, heavily bejeweled hands expressively as he told his tale. He was one of the most successful storytellers in all the southern lands, as his jewels and gaudy robes attested. The children of the rich merchants sat in a little semicircle around the old man's blanket and wriggled in anticipation of his story, for this was only the overture.

"To many lands have we traveled, always searching out the best bazaars, the finest markets, where we sell our wares for the highest prices, then bring our treasures home piled deep in the holds of our golden ships. We fear no one in all the northern or the southern lands. The barbarians of Braegerd Isle may harry our ships, but in the end we conquer them. Were it not for us and our trade, they would not have the wood for their masts, the cloth for their sails, or the ropes for their rigging. Let a single ship of ours be taken by one of theirs and they think it a great victory. Then we raise the price of all our goods and get that ship's value back a hundredfold."

The children laughed and made rude comments about the barbarians of Braegerd Isle. The storyteller smiled indulgently. Their laughter attracted more customers to his stall, more merchants who wanted their children to hear all manner of good things about commerce and barter. For this they paid the old man well with brightly shining vitrics, the most valuable coin in all Vair. The vitrics rang prettily as they cascaded into the blue-enameled brass bowl at the story-teller's feet.

"Now this is a tale," the storyteller went on, smoothing his long white beard, "that happened in the olden days. It began in a place not far from where we now sit. Think of that, my children!"

The children did think of it, and wondered. All around them buzzed and hummed and roared and cackled the great bazaar of Ishma, chief of all bazaars in the known world. It was said that the governor of Ishma had offered two saddlebags of gold to the man who could encircle the market-place in the three days the bazaar was held. The man might ride a horse if he chose. Thus far the gold still awaited a successful claimant.

There was nothing that could not be bought in the great bazaar of Ishma; even the city of Ishma had grown out of the bazaar, not the other way around. Beasts, birds, and fishes of all kinds, alive and dead, might be found at that market. All manner of meat and drink, musical instruments, singers, dancers, readers of poetry—all that might delight the idle hours of men—were for sale here. Slaves sold at Ishma were forever after treated with reverence in the house-holds that bought them, just for being Ishma-ware. Gold, silver, spices, gems, leathers, furs, silks, peacock feathers, dresses made of the scales of iridescent fishes—all hung like so much common laundry in the stalls and shops that joggled one another for place in the great bazaar of Ishma.

The merchants of the bazaar were almost as gaudy as their wares, for most had grown rich through foreign trade. They wore robes of the finest tissue, colored like the sunrise: pink, yellow, salmon, streaks of gold and red and faintest blue. On their heads they wore coronets and caps and northern-style hats and hoods and little turbans, depending on the land where they did most of their trading. Thus if a customer wanted wool from Sombrunia, he looked above the swirling tide of human heads until he saw a merchant wearing Sombrunian headgear. It was better than a sign—for a sign above each stall would take up too much valuable space.

Nobody could describe the smells of the great bazaar of Ishma. Only foot traffic could get through the narrow inner warrens. Accordingly they always smelled strongly of humanity . . . and the tethered horses, camels, donkeys, and ostriches that the shoppers led in to carry home their purchases. Dogs and cats aplenty wandered from one street to the next, mostly favoring the Lane of the Butchermen. Sometimes these free beasts explored as far as the Street of the Pet-Sellers, where their more fortunate cousins reclined among silk cushions, waiting to be bought; sometimes they followed the smell of other animals to the Street of Entertainments, where occasionally an animal trainer would pick up one of the thousand strays and give it a good living as a wise beast. And through the smells of men and animals came the green scents of fresh vegetables, the cool fragrances of ripe fruits and fresh-cut flowers, the exquisite aroma of many spices, the heavy reek of various perfumes and incenses.

"This is a tale," said the old man, "of a young man who lived with his father—a merchant of great importance—in the village of Basha that lies to the east. On low hills it lies, and from the windows of his house the young man could see the mountains."

At this point the children bowed low and muttered hasty prayers. The mountains that surrounded Vair were its safeguard. The sea guards the north, and Vair's fleet is mighty in war; but the mountains are a shield. To the west lives the feared Lord Olian of the Desert Hordes, whose realm is the Desert of Thulain, and farther west is Vahrd, home of a hardy and dangerous barbarian people. The mountains discourage thoughts of invasion. To the south and east lie the lands that few men know. They pose no military threat, but beings more powerful than the men of Vahrd and more ruthless than the hordes of Olian dwell there. The children and their elders regularly pray for the continued protection of the mountains and hope this will suffice.

The storyteller commended their piety. He passed around a wooden bowl of candied fruits and bade them help themselves. The bowl went around the circle and returned empty. The old man laughed and the brilliant sapphires that hung from his ears jiggled and danced in the sunlight.

"Children," he said, suddenly solemn, "this story is not always a pleasant one. You may be frightened and wish to run away. Do not flee, my children, for the tale may grow lighter or grow more filled with terrors still; but if you run away, those who see you run will call you cowards, and so you'll be called for the rest of your lives. Wherefore sit you down, children, and hearken well to what it is I tell you."

Chapter II

DOGGEDLY

In every town, in every village, there is always one boy the neighbors point out and prophesy great or terrible things about. In the years of his growth and young manhood, Mustapha felt he had been needlessly singled out as that boy.

As Mustapha grew older, he learned stealth and cunning worthy of any thief. It was not because he was wicked, but because such skills were useful for overhearing more of what the neighbors said about him. By judicious eavesdropping, he learned that they pitied him. He was the youngest son of his father's third wife, the fifteenth son of the house. He wondered why they pitied him for that and resolved to ask his father.

The old gentleman sighed when Mustapha put that question to him. Mustapha was young yet, and knew little of law or custom.

"My son," said the merchant, "I am wealthy, but were I to divide my estate among all my sons, each would have little. Custom decrees that I must leave my goods to my four eldest sons. You and those of your brothers who receive nothing at my death have . . . choices. I do not care to speak of them."

Mustapha made certain inquiries and learned what choices he had. He could enroll as a slave to one of the four chief brothers, or he could try to kill the eleven brothers who stood between him and the possibility of becoming a chief brother himself. He liked neither alternative.

His other brothers were not so scrupulous. Before his

11

father's death, two of the chief brothers met mysterious ends
and three others suffered from strange stomach pains after
a family banquet. These odd deaths and close calls awoke
Mustapha to the possibility that family life was not the happy
oasis he had thought. A heavy melancholy began to eat at
his heart.

His father found him sunk in bitter meditation beneath
a palm tree and spoke to him. "My child," he said, "I am
old and you are my fifteenth son. Of all my sons, I love
you the best, and yet there is something I must tell you that
tears my heart. Leave, Mustapha. Do not stay to be a slave.
I was my father's sixteenth son, and I fled his house to seek
my fortune by my wits. See what I have amassed today!
Do likewise, and make your own way in the world."

Mustapha was still on the verge of manhood when his
father gave him that advice, so the thought of leaving home
was very large and frightening indeed. If he thought about
it in the daytime, with a scroll on his knees that told of
some hero's adventures, it seemed a tempting thing to do.
If he thought about it in the strangeness of night, however,
even the lot of a slave seemed preferable. So the years passed
and he did nothing.

Day flowed into day and he turned eighteen, receiving
his sword from his father according to custom. Then he was
forced into action. His father and sixth-from-eldest brother,
Jemir, returned home from the great bazaar of Ishma just
as the first evening stars appeared in the tawny twilight. At
the gate of the house his father called for wine. Someone
brought a goblet and he drained it greedily, then fell senseless from the saddle. He was carried to his bed and his
family sent for leeches and wise men; but the healers saw
no hope and suggested that the old man speak to his sons
when he awoke.

He called for Mustapha first. Mustapha knelt by the bed
and wept, but his father laughed and did not seem much
changed from other days.

"It would seem I am dying," he said, a smile on his face.
"Do you remember our talk, these many years past?" His
son nodded. "I told you to go, yet here you stay. Why?"

"I could not bring myself to leave home, Father."

"Home? Fourteen—now twelve—brothers who care only
for themselves? Your mother, may she be at peace, is no

more. You have a house, not a home, here. Houses are plentiful in the world."

"I could not leave you."

"I am pleased," said the old man, patting Mustapha on the head. "I shall not see you again, I think, but while I lived you were a joy to my eyes and the pride of my heart. Now this trifle is all I can give you." He handed his son a small leather bag with a few vitrics in it. "There is nothing left to keep you here anymore. Go with my blessing."

"I shall not go."

"I say you shall. Do you think your brothers will let you watch beside my deathbed? They mistrust each other too much. Go, my son. If you love me, go."

Mustapha leaned close and kissed his father. In later years he spoke often of that final parting. As he drew near to embrace the old man, he thought he heard his father laughing as in the old days. That final laugh, that final kiss of love, enriched his heart and made the desolation of that farewell easier to bear.

His brothers did not notice when Mustapha left. He paused only to stuff a saddlebag with provisions from the kitchen. He took the sword his father had given him, a precious miniature painting of the old man, and a necklace that had belonged to his mother (but which his eldest brother's wife had appropriated).

His horse was displeased when he mounted it and galloped away into the hills beyond Basha without even the formality of a lump of sugar. From the hills he got a pretty clear view of his village. He waited. On the third day he heard a great commotion and saw the smoke of his father's funeral pyre rising black against the dawn. When at last the winds dispersed the smoke, he rode away.

Chapter III

REIGNING CATS
AND DOGS

By the time Mustapha reached Ishma he had spent all his money and had to sell his horse into the bargain. On foot, dirty and weary, he stepped upon the wondrous stones that lead from the highway into the bazaar. It is said that he did not find Ishma marvelous because his eyes were destined to behold greater wonders.

Whether or not he was amazed, one thing was certain: He was very lonely. Hunger of the stomach he still kept at a distance; hunger of the heart was more immediate. He had left all the family he had ever known. Amid so many people, all bursting with noise and chatter and heat and confusion, Mustapha was alone.

Like a riptide, the waves of people in the great bazaar of Ishma did not give him time to realize how truly alone he was. He was carried like a twig in floodwater to wherever the multitude was going. Having no destination, Mustapha allowed himself to drift with the human current until it began to ebb and set him down at last in the Street of the Pet-Sellers.

Only the very rich have pets. Before a beast may enter a house as companion rather than servant, it must be well fed, well groomed, and instructed in manners. The pet-sellers had a profitable business, for a stray looks as fine as a purebred beast if given enough food and love. It brings the same price. The food cost little, the love cost less, and the pet-sellers did very well. It was a mark of status to own a pet, and the market cur that a rich nobleman cuffed today might be sold to his wife as a lapdog on the morrow.

Because pets cost so much, traffic in the Street of the Pet-Sellers was light. It was also located at the border of the bazaar, so many a spoiled lordling or lady would defy the law and come there in a litter or palanquin. As Mustapha passed, he saw an extraordinarily beautiful woman, clothed in gauzes the color of a parrot's plumage and ajingle with gold jewelry, haggling like an old fishwife over the price of a supremely contemptuous calico cat.

"But, Breath of the Eastern Dawn," implored the seller, "I beg of you to reconsider. This lovely and cultured feline will grace your home, attend upon your person, and be a source of envy to your friends and neighbors. Fifteen hundred vitrics!"

"No, Tongue of a Thousand Serpents!" said the lady. "No more than thirteen hundred vitrics will I pay."

"Understand me, Pearl of Infinite Delight," countered the seller. "Rather than sell this queen among her kind for thirteen hundred vitrics, I would sell my own daughters!"

"Then sell them," answered the lady. "Not if the beast were the fabled Queen Nahrit herself, come out of the elder times, would I give a vitric more."

"Surely a man of such wealth as your husband could afford the paltry sum of fourteen hundred vitrics?" the merchant wheedled, letting the lady hold the cat. Puss immediately began to purr, snuggling down in the lady's arms.

"Thief and Son of Thirty Thieves," sighed the lady, stroking the cat, "you have hit upon it. My husband can well afford it, for he leaves me all alone in his palace when he goes abroad to trade. The animal will be honorable company for my lonely heart. In truth, that is all they are good for, their society. The envy of my friends is nothing; a new dress procures it. A pleasing fountain or exquisite vase might grace my house just as well. No, for the company she shall bear me in my long solitudes, I will purchase her."

The merchant clapped. One of his daughters brought coffee and cakes, the better to seal the bargain; the lady passed the cat along to her maid.

There was nothing more to see so Mustapha went his way, but he thought long about what he had overheard. The lady spoke of loneliness, yet what was hers compared with his own? Merely to relieve her solitude she had spent fourteen hundred vitrics on a cat. Dogs cost much more.

"If I only had a cat or dog, or even a small bird, to ease my heart and help me forget my loss," sighed Mustapha. The few coins left to him would buy nothing in the Street of the Pet-Sellers, but at least they would buy him a glass of wine. He turned the corner and searched for a tavern.

There was no Street of Taverns in Ishma. Instead, they were crowded into little holes-in-the-wall throughout the bazaar. Mustapha found one nearby. It was dark and it stank, but the wine was good enough.

"Good evening, friend. You have the look of a man who needs more than one cup of wine." A short, burly fellow with swarthy skin and a scrawny goatee and mustache straddled the stool opposite Mustapha. The man was smiling affably.

Mustapha, glad of company, did not stop to wonder at meeting such a friendly chap in such an unfriendly place. "Another cup of wine would be welcome," he answered, "but my last coin has gone to pay for this one."

"No!" The man gasped and goggled his eyes as if this were the most horrible news he had heard in his life. "It should not be so! Allow me to offer you a cup as payment for intruding on your privacy." He called for the surly waiting-girl to bring them each a flagon. The first flagon vanished and he called for another.

"I cannot let you," Mustapha protested. "I am already in your debt and cannot pay you back."

The dark man smiled. "Let us leave it to fate," he said smoothly, setting a pack of cards on the table. "High card shall do as he pleases." Mustapha nodded. It seemed fair. They cut for high card and the dark man won. "Now you must let me treat you," he grinned. Wine was brought and soon was gone.

"Do you play cards?" Mustapha's new friend asked. "Not just cut them, but really play?"

"At home I did. Playing without stakes is idle, and I have nothing to wager," Mustapha lied. He still held his father's portrait and his mother's necklace. Only death could part him from either.

"A shame," the fellow said, then brightened. "I know! Let us play a single hand, you and I. I have barely more money than you, but I do have a means of earning more. I

have an old dog that is tied up under the tavern bar. I'll
wager him—and if you win, I'll redeem him for five vitrics
from you tomorrow when my master pays me. You will
wager . . . your cap. Agreed?"

Mustapha had drunk so much wine on top of so little
food that he would have agreed to wager his trousers. Through
the fuddlement of wine he saw the dark man deal the cards
and announce that they would play sosral. Wine seemed to
give Mustapha luck, for within a remarkably short time he
found the other man shaking his hand vigorously and congratulating him on a brilliant game.

"Never have I seen a master of sosral like you! Never
seek to become a cardsharp, friend. Your genius will betray
you. Now I'll bring you the dog; I will redeem him tomorrow." The man scuttled away, to return with a dirty
animal on a rope lead. It was small, with floppy, pointed
ears and a nose like a chocolate drop. You could not tell its
color for the dirt.

The loser put the lead in Mustapha's hand and knelt
before the hound. "Light of My Heart, Comfort of My
Desolation, my soul cries out that we must be parted for
even such a short while! But do not fear, Lotus of the World.
I shall return for you, for my heart shall not let me rest until
we are once more together." He wiped his eyes furtively,
got to his feet, and bade Mustapha farewell.

Mustapha watched as the man scurried from the tavern,
then looked down at the dog. "I wish I could keep you,"
he said tenderly. "But I fear it can't be so. Your master is
so eager to redeem you that I am sure he will return with
the money within an hour."

The dog looked up at Mustapha with large, limpid eyes
and remarked, "Are you a fool? He'll never return. I'm all
yours."

Mustapha gaped. The dog went back to its task: chewing
a large and succulent bone that one of the tavern patrons
had dropped. "Did you speak?" asked Mustapha. He prayed
he was only hearing things. The alternative was to think he
had gone mad. Too much wine!

The dog opened its mouth. It seemed to be laughing.
Then it got up and tugged on the lead. Mustapha, thinking
it needed to answer the call of nature, took it out of the

tavern. The dog dragged him up one street and down another until they were out of the great bazaar and in the town of Ishma. Night was falling swiftly. The dog took him to a dark alley and stopped before a certain door. It lifted its hind leg and anointed the door thoroughly.

"That is Izank's door and that is what I think of him!" snorted the dog. "Now, as to whether or not I can talk—"

The dog broke off its discourse; it was useless to go on. Mustapha had collapsed in the street.

Chapter IV

IT SHOULDN'T HAPPEN TO A DOG

The warm, wet tongue of the dog awakened Mustapha. The cur gave a hyena grin and said, "It's about time. I was about to resort to desperate measures. Come on."

Bewildered and aching from his faint onto the cobblestones of the alley, Mustapha followed the dog once more through the winding streets of Ishma. By now it was full night and torches lit the street corners. Music and voices sounded distant in the darkness. Sometimes, as the dog pulled him along, Mustapha passed a brightly lit door and heard the sounds of glasses clinking and merry laughter within. But these inviting doorways soon became fewer and less frequent. Even the sounds of distant celebration dissolved into the silence of the night. No torches brightened these street corners and Mustapha had to grope like a blind man whither the dog would lead him. At last they stopped and Mustapha sat down.

The moon rose like a bright, new-minted fier and Mustapha saw that he was seated on a low hillock just beyond the town. It was sandy, for desert covers most of Vair, but the hillock was sparsely covered with patches of tough, short grass, a comfortable resting place. In the moonlight the dog looked like a shadow.

"Aren't you going to ask me my story?" it demanded. Its mouth was open, tongue lolling, in an expression most uncannily like a mocking laugh. Mustapha felt a twinge of annoyance at the brute's sarcastic look.

"I am waiting for you to begin it," he said.

"Very well, I will," said the dog, still leering. "I was

born . . . no, no, that's not what interests you. Friend, you have been duped. Aye, swindled, deceived, and greatly put upon by a misbegotten rogue. You are not the first, for Izank the Maleficent is a name to conjure with in certain unsavory quarters of society. This same Izank, whom you thought you ruined in that game of cards, has won untold thousands of vitrics in similar matches."

"A man's luck may change," Mustapha offered, weakly.

"Luck," said the dog, "enters not into Izank's cards. Yet swindling at cards is not his only means of support. He picks pockets, tells fortunes, waylays travelers, and indulges in assassination for a price. Ah, I almost forgot! He also fancies himself a performer, and as such he thought to earn an honest living, against his old age. So he purchased me and trained me, using more cruelty than patience. My small size and his large whip prevented me from tearing his throat out, which he deserved. What could I do to strike back at such a master? If I would not perform, he would not feed me. Oh, he was very ready with punishment, my old master!"

The dog gnashed his teeth at hosts of invisible Izanks. "I bided my time. We traveled to many lands to show off my tricks and earn Izank his brandy money. One day we came to the fair northern port of Cymweh."

"Cymweh!" breathed Mustapha. "I have read of Cymweh. I should like to see it someday."

"It is not as impressive as Ishma"—the dog shrugged— "but it will do. As I was saying, to Cymweh we came and sought a tavern in which to perform. Near the docks was a promising place called the Merry Manticore. We entered, and the rich display we saw there confirmed my master's greedy desires. He jerked my lead and showed me the whip and the stout cane he carried, giving me to understand that if I did not do my best, I would get a double helping of both.

"A space was cleared for us. The patrons were all young and fair of face, all dazzling with jewels and robed in supernatural splendor. I do not remember when it happened, but somehow, in the midst of my dancing act, I tripped and blundered into a little table that held a tray of glasses. These unfortunately spilled into the lap of a noble lady.

"My master had planned to beg a reward from the audience directly after my act. How could he now, when I'd drenched one of the most finely dressed ladies there? In his rage, he hit my back again and again with his whip and cane. I staggered and fell under the blows, but still he whipped me without mercy. Abruptly, it stopped. I thought I had died from the beating, because the next moment I was being placed on a silk cushion and a bowl of dainty meats was set before me by the lady I had offended. Above all I heard the most delicious music in the world: the screams of Izank.

"The scoundrel hung by his robes from a chandelier, writhing as if a thousand imps were tormenting him. And so they were! The Merry Manticore is the tavern of witches and sorcerers in Cymweh. When Izank beat me, they arose against him in a black and awesome cloud of hate. They loosed their enchantments all at once, and it took some time before they ultimately sorted out which spells had fallen upon him and which upon me. Meantime he hung like a fat sausage while the invisible familiars of a score of sorcerers plied clever fingers to his discomfort.

"Among them was a most powerful magician called Ayree. He was young, but strong in his magics. Never did I see such a purebred man! He hailed from north of the northern lands, where all they eat is ice and snow. Ayree it was who sorted out the spells.

"'First,' he said, 'I sense that one of you has punished this tyrant with a spell stronger than the minor tortures of our invisible allies.' A pretty witch admitted she had made a magic condemning Izank to die if he mistreated me again. Another mage said his spell called for Izank's death if he caused mine. 'Furthermore,' said Ayree, 'I have given this dog the gift of speech, so that he may call for help should this rogue threaten him.'

"'And I,' announced a very young sorceress, 'have outdone you all!' When they asked what she meant, she laughed sweetly and said, 'I have given him the ability to put on human shape. If this villain tries to harm him, he can turn into a man himself and thrash this pig to death, if it pleases him.'

"Izank grew pale and so dispirited that the unseen hands could hardly make him twitch any more. The magic makers took him down from the chandeliers, called off their familiars, and booted him out the door. They ordered him to wait for me outside, for I was his dog and if he abandoned me he would surely die.

"A very cold and stiff fellow was Izank when next I saw him. I passed a pleasant night in the tavern, he a terrible one in the chilly street. Fearing for his life, from then on he cared for me as if for an infant prince, but in my heart I still hated him. He didn't enjoy our changed life together, either.

"One night, he had an idea. 'While you are my dog,' he said, 'I must protect you or I perish. If you were the dog of a new master, the spell would be broken for me. There is no love lost between us.' I bit him, to agree, and he had to bear it. 'I see,' said he through clenched teeth, 'that you are of the same opinion. So I shall pass you, curse and all, along to some fool who thinks you just an ordinary dog, and blast the day I ever plucked you from the dunghill!' You, friend, are the lucky winner of Izank's prize and curse."

The dog threw back its head and howled at the moon for joy. Plainly the beast did not love men much and it was enjoying fully the trick played on a hated man-creature. Therefore it shocked the dog more than any curse or kick when Mustapha gently rested his hand upon its head and scratched its ears in a delightful way.

"First, my friend, we shall give you a bath," Mustapha was saying. "The dogs of my father's house always enjoyed a bath. Then I shall gather some twigs and brush you, and then I will make you a more suitable lead. I'll have to use rags, but someday I'll buy you a fine lead of soft leather . . . unless you would prefer your freedom, though it would break my heart to lose you."

"What?" snarled the dog, showing a double row of teeth. "What are you up to? Don't try anything! I'm wise to your tricks! I wasn't Izank's cur all these years without learning how you men operate. Remember the curse!"

"Izank's curse is my blessing," Mustapha said softly, again reaching out and stroking the dog's head. He then explained his own story to the dog, and ended by saying, "I was alone and the gods brought you to me. I was without family or friends and they caused me to meet Izank in the tavern. Stay with me if you will, or else I shall take you to the finest shop in the Street of the Pet-Sellers and leave you there. You shall end your days as the pampered pet and darling of some noble household, and I shall pray to all the gods that Izank's curse remain with me. If any harm befall you, let it mean my own death. You have suffered enough in your lifetime. Now speak your will and it shall be mine."

It was as if the dog had heard Mustapha stop speaking like a man and commence barking like a dog. In a moment the animal had leaped into the young man's arms and was bathing his face with warm, damp kisses, at the same time trying to hug him with all four paws. Then, just as suddenly, the dog sprang away and began to dance and turn somersaults in the moonlight. It only ceased these mad capers from time to time in order to run back to Mustapha and cover his face with doggy kisses again. Exhausted at last, it came and sat before Mustapha, tail wagging.

"May bones bestrew your doorstep and rats be ever plentiful for your hunting!" cried the dog. "You are my master henceforth and I am your slave. If you will remove my lead, I shall never run away, not though I should have to nip the heels of all the demons of the Lands of Wonder to be at your side! O, my master, in token of your love for me and mine for you, give me a name!"

His heart overflowing, Mustapha solemnly considered what to name his dog. "I shall call you Elcoloq," he said at last, "for such was the name of a wondrously wise dog who lived, they say, in the ancient times. He was a hero's dog, but I fear you shall not be so honored in your master. Truly I have not two fiers with which to buy us breakfast."

"Don't worry," said the dog. "Sleep and take your ease. It isn't morning yet. We are not even halfway through the night. A lot of things can happen between a sunset and a dawn."

The dog Elcoloq snuggled its nose under Mustapha's arm and the two companions were soon sleeping together under the bright stars that shone upon Ishma.

Chapter V

DOG STAR

Of the adventures of Mustapha and his wise dog, Elcoloq, a man could speak for seven lifetimes. They wandered together for years over the face of most of the known world. Mustapha lost his first youth and came into full manhood. He was a handsome man, his face burned dark by the sun and made rough by rain and cold. But the elements worked in vain to coarsen him: His deep brown eyes had the same look of kindliness, and the thick growth of his raven beard could not hide the beauty of his mouth. He had grown tall and slender on the road, strong as any soldier who marches dawn to dusk and must look out for himself.

Such was Elcoloq's love for Mustapha that he willingly performed all the tricks that Izank had beaten into him. As traveling players they did not earn much, but Elcoloq was a dog of infinite resource. For many years Mustapha did not know how it happened that the two of them always seemed to have plenty of money, even when he was sure that he had spent their last coin. One day he learned the truth.

They were sleeping in a stable adjacent to the Pig and Castle tavern. This inn stood well to the north of Lyf, where King Ghen, father of King Marn, ruled. Lyf had bitterer winters than any other of the northern lands; because, some say, of the evil spells of those who inhabit the regions even farther north.

Mustapha did not mind the cold. He had plenty of straw to wrap himself in. He did wish for a long woolen tunic and hose besides, but though Elcoloq's antics had earned a goodly sum that very night, it was by no means enough for such an outfit.

Toward the middle of the night, Mustapha awoke to the icy touch of a sharp wind. Someone had opened the stable door and come in. Mustapha, grown used to such things in his long years on the road, grasped his knife under the straw and waited. The horses shifted uneasily and stamped in the darkness.

Mustapha heard the rustle of feet in the straw near his head. When they were near enough, he flipped himself over and toppled the intruder to the ground. Finding the scruff of the footpad's neck, he hauled him to his feet in the dark and pressed his knife uncomfortably close to the fellow's windpipe. Mustapha managed to light the small oil lamp that hung in the stable in order to see the face of his silent enemy.

"An infant assassin!" Mustapha sputtered when he saw the beardless face of a boy staring back at him.

"Master," begged the lad, who was not more than eleven or twelve years old, "do not kill me."

"I don't hurt babies," Mustapha snapped. "Not even when they seek to rob me and slay me in the night."

"Nay, master," said the boy, his large brown eyes brimful of sincerity. "I come to serve you, not to slay you. Behold the gift I bring for you." Onto the straw at Mustapha's feet he tossed a pouch of red chamois stamped with gold designs. The strings by which the purse used to hang from a rich man's belt had been cut as prettily as you please. "There is much gold for you, master."

"And why should you bring me gold? Who am I to you or you to me that you fetch me such wealth?" Mustapha demanded.

"I am your most faithful and loyal servant," said the boy, and melted from Mustapha's hands. Elcoloq grinned up at his master from the stable floor.

Mustapha had never before seen Elcoloq change his shape. He had long forgotten that one of the wizards at the Merry Manticore had given the dog the ability to do so at will. At last he understood where the extra money had come from. How many times before this Elcoloq must have become a boy and in his human shape scoured the streets for likely victims of his skill as a cutpurse!

"That will do!" said Mustapha sternly. Elcoloq merely wagged his tail and leered. "You shall not assume that shape again for such wicked purposes, even if it means that I must starve."

"I hear, master," said the dog, "but I don't think I will obey."

"You must!"

"Master, I obey you in all else, but I will never see you go hungry and cold if I can prevent it. This night's work brings you enough gold to buy warmer clothing. If my small skill can bring you comfort, I will use it in spite of you."

"And you will incur my displeasure!"

"Oh, no, master. I doubt it," said the dog. He turned around three times in the straw and went to sleep under the glowering gaze of his master.

When the following day dawned, Mustapha had reached a decision. He woke Elcoloq, gave him breakfast, then informed him of the plan.

"Two choices are mine if I am to reform you from your life as a scoundrel," he said. "Either I must become so rich that you will nevermore need to abuse your wondrous gift of transformation, or else we must have you cured of this ability. It must be one or the other, or one of these fine days I will hear that you have been caught and hanged for your thieveries."

"Well, master," said Elcoloq, "which shall it be?"

"That," Mustapha sighed, "I cannot say. I have heard of many spells in the Twelve Kingdoms. Some can be lifted, some cannot. I do not know what sort of a spell you have upon you. It was no simple enchantment, but part of a volley of magics; that makes it difficult. As to riches, we shall have to see what fortune brings us in our travels."

"There is one thing we could try," the dog ventured.

"Speak, wise one."

"Why don't we find Ayree?"

"Ayree? Ah, yes! The young warlock. I should like to meet that powerful enchanter, Elcoloq. But how do we find him? Must we go to Cymweh and await his return to the tavern where you met him? Cymweh lies far to the south."

The dog gave a short, yapping laugh. "We do well if we seek Ayree, master. He lives to the north of the northernmost lands, it is said. Already we are north, and very close to his abode."

"But north of the known lands live . . . well, no one knows exactly what lives to the north," protested Mustapha.

"I have already told you that Ayree lives there," said the dog. "Of course, we can always forget all about it and go on as we've been doing."

"Never!" Mustapha stormed. "Very well, we have no choice. Not unless I find a sack of gems under this straw, anyway. So let us seek this Ayree, that he may disenchant you."

They left the stable of the Pig and Castle and found a tailor's shop. Here Mustapha spent what he hoped would be the last gold Elcoloq would bring him illegally. In place of the lighter robes of the south he donned a long, warm, coffee-colored wool tunic and hose. He had enough cash left over to buy a second-quality hooded cloak trimmed with scraggly bits of ancient fox fur and a little blanket coat for Elcoloq.

Snow lay everywhere upon the ground, upon the trees, upon the houses. The faint sunlight cast blue shadows against the drifts. The wind blew gently, lifting up a flurry of powder-fine flakes to dance silver in the sunlight. In the fleeting summertime of that kingdom a road led north, but now it was hidden beneath the snowfall until spring.

"Road or no road, what does it matter?" Mustapha shrugged fatalistically. "We go to a place that has no roads at all, so let us start with none." Elcoloq sniffed the thin air of the north and set the direction and the pace.

Some say that the lands of the north are the lands of sorcery. Certainly they are not the lands of men. But the poor and the weary of the world will sometimes wander into these unfriendly regions. Mustapha and Elcoloq saw an occasional hut in their travels, although mostly they found vast desolations of ice and snow, marked only with the light print of a snowrabbit's paws. Once Mustapha thought he saw a stag, as white as the snow it moved upon. It looked more like a ghost than an earthly stag to Mustapha's southern eyes.

Men who bargained in the pelts of beasts would meet Mustapha and his wise dog in the snowy wilderness and

trade a bit of food for a little entertainment and a tale of
the southern lands. These brushes with other men kept the
two adventurers going, for in all their travels Mustapha had
not been able to bring down the smallest of rabbits with his
bow.

The farther north they went, the fewer men they met.
Mustapha's beard grew long and ragged; Elcoloq had to
wear shreds of cloth wrapped around his paws to save them
from freezing. At night they huddled together in the small
tent Mustapha had purchased from a northern trader. The
one mercy of the north was that even the winds appeared
to have frozen. Eventually their supplies ran out.

The sun shone hard and white as ice over the featureless
snowbound plain. Not a single spiral of smoke betrayed the
camp of a trapper or wanderer. So vicious was the frost that
Mustapha and Elcoloq no longer had to wade through drifts,
for the snow no sooner fell than froze to the hardness of
packed earth. It made for easier walking, but unless some
chance of food showed itself, they would not be able to go
much farther.

"My good Elcoloq," murmured Mustapha, trudging after
the dog, "why do you hurry? We have no idea where we
are going, unless into the shadows."

The dog bounded on ahead of his master, then turned
and trotted back to hearten him. "Your nose has frozen, but
not mine," he said. "We are not abandoned yet. Come!"

Mustapha, weary and cold, swapped his bow and bag
from one shoulder to the other. He followed Elcoloq as he
would have followed a snow-spirit, so weak had his will
become.

The endless snow had dulled Mustapha's eyes; he saw
everything through an uncaring glare of whiteness. Suddenly
he blinked and stared. There was something different ahead
of them, a sign that they had gone too long without seeing.
A wisp of gray trailed slowly up the sky, and from far away
Mustapha thought he scented the aroma of roasting meat.
Elcoloq yipped his joy and raced across the snow. Mustapha
stumbled after him.

They stopped their flight on the brow of a gentle hill
overlooking a shallow depression in the otherwise flat ter-
rain. A lodge of skins, such as the trappers used in their

deep-winter camps, was cradled there, the smoke rising from a hole in the roof. Together man and dog slid down the hill until they stood before the flap of hide that served as the door.

Mustapha raised his hands to clap, the only way of knocking when there was no wooden door. A growl from Elcoloq made him hesitate. He had only heard that note once before: On a summer's eve in Glytch, as he was lazing beside the Opalza Sea, Elcoloq had growled in just that way and made a sudden spring to seize and kill the venomous sand-colored dune snake that was coiled and ready to strike.

"Master, I distrust this place," snarled the dog between his clenched fangs.

"Elcoloq, why should you? It's got the look of a hospitable house, and we must get food or we cannot go on."

"Hospitable? Many traps look hospitable. I do not think I like whatever lives here."

Mustapha grew impatient. The scent of cooking was too tantalizing to his empty belly for him to pass this place by on a dog's whim. He clapped his hands sharply and a muffled voice answered him. In a moment, the hide curtain was pulled back and a shapely white arm beckoned to them.

A blazing fire in the center of the lodge cast shadows over the piles of furs and supplies that lay scattered in the corners. By the fire's light Mustapha saw the owner of the lodge and immediately lost his power of speech.

She was as fair as a royal lady, hair and skin white as southern water-blossom, eyes blue as shadows on the snow. A long robe of scarlet wool, caught in at the waist with a belt of steel discs, revealed her youthful figure and her grace, but she had about her the air of a wild thing as she studied Mustapha and his wise dog.

"Who are you?" she demanded. A thin dagger flashed in her hand, a weapon more suitable for a palace assassin than for one living in the northern wastes. "What do you want?"

"Fair one, I am Mustapha, a humble player, and this is the good dog whose tricks earn me my bread. We ask for a little food, nothing more."

"A player! You lie. For what audience do you play here?"

"Lovely princess, I do not lie. I confess I am as surprised

to see a lady of your beauty here, where there are no young lords to compete for your hand, as you are to find a player where there are no audiences."

"I am Bilka, daughter of the trapper Ogin. My father is dead and I follow his trade," she said, her face hard. "Now tell me truth, if there is any truth in you. What do you seek here, player?"

Mustapha folded his arms on his breast and bowed. "You are wise," he said. "I do not lie. I am a player, but another business calls me here. I seek the warlock prince."

"Ayree?" the girl snapped. "You are a fool! You are not the first to blunder here searching for a dream. Return to your home, player, and earn your living there. Nothing lies to the north of Bilka's house but death."

Mustapha was downcast at her words. Seeing his sorrow, Bilka changed her tone and laid aside her dagger. Like a wraith of falling snow she glided across the floor toward him, the hem of her scarlet gown brushing the hardened carpet of eternal white.

"Stay here the night, good Mustapha," she crooned. "Stay here with me and refresh yourself. It is a long, hard way to the southern lands from here. Stay, and leave me when you like. I have food and drink aplenty for you. I have robes of peerless white, softer than love itself. Stay, Mustapha, stay."

Mustapha felt his eyelids grow heavy as the beautiful maiden drew close, twining her cool white arms around his neck. Her eyes burned with strange blue flames, and her mouth was wide and very red. He bent forward to kiss her and taste her red, red mouth.

With a bark, Elcoloq bounded forward and bit his master fairly on the leg—not a deep bite, but enough to make him cry out and spring backward. Bilka too sprang away from the crazed animal, her sharp little teeth chattering angry words in an unknown language.

"Forgive me, my lady, I don't know why—" Mustapha began, seizing Elcoloq by the collar and pulling him away from Bilka.

"Take him out! Take him out!" shrieked the girl. "There is a coil of rope by the door. Tie him outside at once!"

Elcoloq did not look at all repentant as Mustapha tied him to a hook used for hanging fresh pelts on the outside of the lodge. It puzzled Mustapha mightily. The dog had always been loving to him. The attack hurt him worse in his heart than in his leg.

"Elcoloq, what came over you?" he asked.

"Shh," the dog cautioned. "We don't want your new friend to know I can talk. It would ruin all her plans. Go back to her, Mustapha, but keep her at arm's length. She is no more a trapper's daughter than I am a dancing girl. Her kiss would freeze your blood, my master. She is evil."

"The long journey has made you mad," said Mustapha, indignant at these slurs against the lovely maiden.

"Test my madness, then. Where are the tracks of a trapper's sled and his dogs? Where are fresh skins? Where do you see even a pair of snowshoes, such as usually hang beside a true trapper's door? Besides all this, my master, I smelled something else inside that lodge. She roasts rabbits merely to cover the smell of her true food. She is a snow-spirit, an evil creature, and she has captured a child."

"I cannot believe that," replied Mustapha, but he made no move to return to the lodge. Rather, he untied Elcoloq from the pelt hook and told him, "I will trust you to stay here on your own word. It is not right to punish you when you thought you were helping me. But stay!" He turned and went back inside.

Bilka was waiting for him, all her fright melted into loving looks and sighs. A steaming dish of rabbit lay on the floor beside a thick carpet. "Eat, Mustapha, and be strong," she said, guiding him to sit and joining him on the floor.

"Do you eat nothing?" he asked. The rabbit had a succulent smell that almost made him forget common courtesy. No well-bred man would eat without first bidding his host to join him.

"I do not care for rabbit," she replied, smiling. "Eat, and I will entertain you, player. I will sing you a northern song and ask for my own reward."

She took up a stringed instrument of a kind he had never seen and played a low, wailing melody, melancholy as the wind through the winter pines. Her song was unintelligible, sung in a language of silver, the words lost and unimportant. The melody was all. She finished and set down the instrument.

"And now my reward," she said, leaning toward him. "Kiss me, Mustapha."

He hung back, thinking of what Elcoloq had said. They sat close to the fire, so close that he could not say if the piles of objects inside the lodge were real or illusory, shades of things that one might expect to find in a trapper's lodge. The wind soughed around the outside of the house, a wind in a place where there should be none, and a remote sound insinuated itself through the honeyed curtain of Bilka's words.

"What's that?" cried Mustapha, scrambling to his feet.

"What, my love?" asked Bilka, arising beside him and placing one cool hand on his neck. "I hear nothing."

"It sounded like a child crying. I heard it."

"There are no children here, love," she said. "Kiss me, and abandon dreams."

He put her gently away from him and insisted, "I heard a child, I say." He stepped outside the swimming circle of firelight and began to hunt among the bales of pelts in the semidarkness. Three corners of the lodge yielded nothing. His hand was outstretched to move a pack of brown furs when Bilka's voice rang out in a shriek that chilled him to the bone.

"Touch it not! She is mine!"

He wheeled about and faced a transformation of horror. The sweet-faced maiden was gone; in her place there raged a gaunt and ghostly hag, her stringy white hair flying wildly around her head in a tempest of her own creation. Snow blew from her taloned hands and her blue eyes were smudged hollows in a papery skull.

"Touch it not! One hand upon her and you are a dead man!" The creature came for him, preceded by a frosty blast of wind that nearly threw Mustapha to the ground. In her right claw reappeared the slender dagger, now made of purest ice and as deadly as a serpent.

Mustapha cast about him for some weapon to use against the snow-beast. Her fury had dissolved the illusions of the lodge; pelts and campfire were gone. Only a tiny bundle lay whimpering at Mustapha's feet and he knew he must protect it, no matter the cost.

In an instant the creature was on him. Mustapha's hands were his only weapon against the spawn of glacier and blizzard, so thrusting one hand beneath the flying hair, he sought the monster's throat.

Numbness pierced his shoulder and closed around his hand at the same moment. The snow-beast cried in awful exultation and raised the bloodstained ice-dagger for a second thrust. This time she meant to have his heart. The hand that had touched her stung as if it had been plunged into ice water. Mustapha had no defense against the final assault.

He closed his eyes, waiting for death, even hoping for the silence of it to blot from his ears the horrible cackling laugh of the monster. Then a familiar sound broke through his consciousness, the voice of Elcoloq in full throat. The frigid talon at his throat slacked its grip and the snow-beast was thrown backward off his body by the impact of the little dog's charge. Snapping, snarling, howling his anger, Elcoloq sent the creature rolling. The ice-dagger fell from its claw with the shock.

Mustapha snapped it up at once and leaped to his feet, lunging after Elcoloq. The wise dog suspected what would happen if he bit the monster, so contented himself with keeping it at bay by growls and empty snaps until his master could join him in the fight. In the darkness of the lodge they waged their battle, man and dog against the evil one, and at last the hideous apparition raised one skeletal arm to strike down Elcoloq. It was the move Mustapha had been waiting for. With the wild battle cry of his native land he threw the icy dagger straight and true. A revolting smell filled the tent as thick, bluish liquid ran down the monster's arm from the wound. It uttered a soul-sickening cry before it sank down and seemed to lose all pretense of solid form, liquefying and soaking back into the snow from which it came.

Elcoloq and Mustapha, both panting, exchanged a look before falling into a mutual embrace. The dog licked his master's frostbitten hand, trying to restore it to warmth and life. The flesh was almost black, the nails as gray as a dead man's. It had no feeling at all.

"No matter," said Mustapha, trying to hide the pain that licked tongues of flame up from the withered hand to wash his left side with agony. "We live. Let us release the child that this creature held captive and be on our way."

Accordingly, obeying his master, Elcoloq trotted over to retrieve the bundle that had whimpered and given the snow-beast away. It was gone. Save for themselves, the lodge was empty.

"It was not a big child, judging from the size of the bundle," said Mustapha. "Could it have run away?"

Elcoloq ran outside to look for spoor, but found none. The spirits of the air might have snatched the little one away for all he knew. There was nothing outside but snow.

"We cannot stay here and search," said Mustapha. "Let us go on. Lead me, Elcoloq." He shouldered their meager pack and left the evil lodge behind forever.

Elcoloq was a perceptive beast. It did not take him long to notice that his master's pace had slowed considerably and that the man no longer shifted his pack from shoulder to shoulder. The dead hand hung heavily at the end of Mustapha's left arm and breathed the breath of sickness over the young man's entire body. Elcoloq was troubled and confused by all this. If he paused to let Mustapha catch up, his master told him to go on and pretended there was nothing wrong. Beads of sweat on the southerner's brow sparkled like a princely diadem in the arctic sunlight.

The charade vanished with the last of Mustapha's strength. Elcoloq turned and saw no sign of his master. Backtracking a bit, he found Mustapha outstretched in the snow, the black-ened hand as stiff as if carved from ebony. Licking Mustapha's face did no good. Gentle nips at clothing or flesh did not rouse him. Raw panic seized the dog and he pointed his nose skyward in a long-drawn howl of utter despair.

In mid-howl he stopped, pricking up his ears to the north, from where a rushing sound had suddenly come. If it was a wind, if the sleeping demons of the tempest had awakened and were lashing a blizzard toward the dog and his helpless master, then they were as good as dead. The sound of fiercely blowing winds grew louder, then abruptly stopped.

Elcoloq's curiosity was aroused. What storm came on and then turned back in its course? Whatever had made that blustering sound might be far more dangerous than a storm. With a last glance at his prostrate master, the dog bounded off to investigate.

He had not gone far when he found himself in another world, another universe. The sun shone, and a twin sun shared the sky with it. The dog stared at the unnatural twin in the heavens, then saw another dog, his own twin, staring at him. Elcoloq growled and pranced up to the other dog in stiff-legged challenge. Move for move, the dog responded to the dare. This was too much for Elcoloq. He snarled and charged the interloper. Snarling back with equal ferocity, the other dog charged too. They met with a hollow thud and Elcoloq recled back, stunned. He had run at full speed into a titanic wall of ice.

Tinkling laughter, like ice crackling in the spring thaw, sounded high above him. Elcoloq looked up and saw that the ice wall belonged to a gigantic castle, built all of the glittering substance, and upon whose battlements a troupe of beautiful maidens had assembled. They pointed to Elcoloq, giggling at the dog's attack on his own reflection. He could count eleven of the flaxen-haired maidens. A twelfth joined them to see what all the merriment was about. When she saw Elcoloq she smiled, but the smile quickly faded when the smallest maiden whispered something in her ear.

"Where is the man?" she called down to Elcoloq. "Where is your master, good dog?"

For answer Elcoloq barked and made a short run back in the direction where Mustapha's body lay. He had already encountered one monster in the guise of a lovely women, and here were possibly twelve similarly masked terrors. He played the part of common dog, hiding his gift of speech.

Each of the ladies spread her azure cloak to the unseen breezes, each one let the invisible forces waft her to the snowy ground. They descended as gracefully as swans, then the eldest knelt beside Elcoloq and kissed him. Her lips were too warm to belong to a creature of snow.

"Good dog," she whispered, "we know you can talk. The child your dear master saved was our smallest sister. Is your master hurt? Take us to him that we may help him."

The kindly voice melted Elcoloq's resolve. "Follow me!" he cried, springing ahead. "Bring blankets and a sled! The snow-beast has stricken his hand with her poisonous cold and driven ice too close to his heart. Hurry!"

Dreams of endless caves of somber ice haunted Mustapha. He imagined himself standing at the mouth of a frozen labyrinth into which he plunged, pursuing a phantom woman. In the center of the maze he found her and kissed her, a kiss that shot untellable cold throughout his body. In his left hand he held a weighty sword of blackest stone and could not let it fall. Then the woman broke away from him and raced on into one of the many branching corridors of her wintry lair. He followed, then lost her, coming into a long, narrow, low-ceilinged room. There a tall, sere man, robed in iron and gray, awaited him. The vision raised his head and Mustapha knew that he was looking into the eyes of Morgeld himself, colder than any creature of snow.

He awakened with a shout of terror and found himself lying in a swiftly moving sled, covered with silver furs and thick comforters. Elcoloq sat to one side of him; to the other sat a golden girl who held his injured hand between white bandages of the softest linen. With a start he realized that he actually could feel the softness of the cloth around the frozen hand. The pain had gone and sensation was returning to it.

The sled passed over the snow like a bird in flight, slowing at last when they approached the wall of ice that had so surprised Elcoloq. When the sled stopped, the fair one who tended Mustapha whistled a dancing tune up toward the crystal battlements where her eleven sisters watched and waited.

The tallest maid looked down and smiled. "Welcome, wanderers, to Castle Snowglimmer," she cried. "Enter and enjoy the hospitality of our house."

The sled began to move again. Feeling stronger, Mustapha sat up; he gasped to see that no beast was harnessed to the front of it. The sled glided on under its own power, following a path around the wall of ice until it arrived at the gate of Snowglimmer. The gate was all of icicles, resplendent in the sunshine. A bent old porter with very bright eyes and very red cheeks admitted them and called for servants to fetch a litter for Mustapha.

"That is not needful," Mustapha said, swinging himself out of the sled against the protests of his sweet nurse. He held up his hand and exclaimed with pleasure to see the first hint of healthy color returning to it. Elcoloq barked joyfully and frisked around his master's feet.

"Follow me to the great hall, Mustapha," said the maiden who had ridden in with them. He bowed agreement and was conducted inside, where the eleven other maidens awaited, prettily arrayed in gowns the color of a sunny winter sky, with trims of ermine. In two lines they stood, six and six when the eldest took her place among them. At sight of Mustapha and Elcoloq each line moved gracefully forward to greet them. They could not be anything but sisters, for each face was of the same creamy whiteness as the next, each had the same snow-pinked cheeks and lips, each the same cerulean eyes; the same golden hair to the waist. The oldest looked about seventeen, and the others followed at intervals of a year or so down to the youngest, who was six.

The oldest curtsied and said, "Noble guests, we are in your debt. You have saved our youngest sister from death. The lord of Castle Snowglimmer would like to welcome you himself. I pray you, follow me." Like a snowflake she drifted through a nearby doorway. Mustapha and Elcoloq went after her, followed in turn by the eleven other maidens.

Mustapha felt great wonder at moving through a palace made entirely of winter. Passing from room to room, he carefully studied the marvels of the icy edifice. The great hall lay close to the outer castle wall and was made of blocks of frosted ice. Sun streamed in so freely through the pellucid walls that no windows were needed. As they penetrated deeper into the castle, the walls changed: Now they went through a room made of clear ice, so clear that it was nigh impossible to see the walls; now they entered a room carved from the blue heart of an iceberg, unseen lights illuminating through the walls, until it seemed a giant, hollow sapphire. Doors did not separate the rooms, but only open archways, sometimes hung with lacy curtains made of beads of ice.

At last they stopped at the first real door Mustapha had yet seen in Castle Snowglimmer. It was a massive double door, apparently made of an uncommonly white wood. Only in laying his hand upon it did Mustapha discover that it was solid silver cast into the semblance of wood.

The oldest maiden opened the silver door onto darkness, knelt toward the lightless interior of the room, and said, "O my brother! We pray you bid welcome to these pilgrims, in the name of all strangers in need and for the sake of their brave rescue of our sister."

An answer came from the blackness, speaking in tones of grim majesty: "What is their purpose here? What brought them to the lodge of the snow-beast? Let them speak and explain themselves!"

Elcoloq took a few steps forward, wagging his tail and sniffing the dank air that the darkened room breathed forth. Mustapha, pushed by the eleven maids behind him, also came forward and said, "O powerful lord! My dog and my own unworthy self have come to these northern regions seeking the dwelling place of the sorcerer Ayree."

"A worthless wretch!" boomed the unseen voice. "How am I to know that the snow-beast was not in league with him? Like all sorcerers, Ayree is Morgeld's creature. Would you risk your lives to come after such a mountebank and knave, were you not already also in the pay of the evil one, Helagarde's wicked lord!"

Elcoloq stopped sniffing and growled, ready to attack the thing that lurked in the darkened room. Mustapha knelt and restrained him.

"I am sure," he said placatingly, "that your noble lordship has his reasons for this poor opinion of Ayree. We have proof of his kindness. I beg you to believe that neither he nor we have anything to do with the cursed master of Helagarde, may it be destroyed forever!"

"Villain!" the voice roared out as from a brazen trumpet. "Do you dare defend Ayree before me? Do you want to learn what becomes of those who speak well of the worthless, low, unspeakably vile Ayree in my house?"

This was too much for Elcoloq. With a single bound he tore himself free from Mustapha and bolted into the pitchy blackness, his jaws snapping. Unthinking, Mustapha went after him, followed by the twelve maidens. The darkened room became a chaos of barks, shrieks, and scuffles.

And then the lights burst out upon them, revealing a room which, for very luxury and beauty, put the others to shame. The walls were of greenest ice, taken from the frozen soul of a wave, and upon them were delicate tracings and inset bas-reliefs on blocks of white ice. Silver flambeaux shed light over it all. The floors were covered with the silvery pelts of beasts unknown to earth, though legends spoke of creatures bearing such furs that might be hunted between the stars. A high ebony throne set with moonstones rested on a dais of ice, and on that throne sat laughing a most handsome young man, fair haired and light eyed like his sisters. In his lap, frantically wagging his tail, sat El-coloq.

"Welcome to Castle Snowglimmer," the young man said. "And welcome, too, in the name of the scoundrel Ayree, who is such a heartless practical joker. Who are you, sir, that you defend me so heartily to myself? Your companion I remember from the Merry Manticore, but you are not the same creature who so mistreated him."

"I am Mustapha of Vair," said Elcoloq's master, bowing before the warlock prince. "We come to ask a favor of you."

"Speak on. I owe you a great service, Mustapha. Understand and forgive the playacting I have put you through. When my smallest sister was taken by the snow-beast, I knew it meant terrible things, even more terrible than the crime itself. I rule these northern wastes and my magics are strong, yet in spite of my powers this malignant spirit entered my domain and dared to come within the charmed circle of my private grounds. The snow-beast is a cowardly monster. She does not like to take risks. Some greater evil lies behind her new courage. I fear to name it."

Mustapha's left hand throbbed again as he thought over Ayree's words. What great evil was this, that could command the nightmare creatures of the wilds? Mustapha's fevered dream returned, the vision of the ashen face and tall figure of Morgeld, lord of cursed Helagarde. Evil winds blew from around the amethyst towers of Helagarde, and no man could tell how mighty was Morgeld. Surely, however powerful he had become, his force could not reach so far north as Ayree's stronghold, thought Mustapha. If that were true, the Twelve Kingdoms rested on a ledge of shifting sands above a bottomless abyss of evil.

"Let us talk of more pleasant things!" Ayree broke in upon Mustapha's thoughts. "Tell me why it is you have come seeking me and I will oblige you."

Mustapha laid one hand reverently upon his breast and told Ayree all the tale of Elcoloq's misadventures in human form. Ayree listened intently, then said they should discuss the matter more thoroughly after a good meal. Ayree's twelve sisters, apprentice sorceresses all, conducted Mustapha and Elcoloq to a sumptuous chamber. Despite its icy walls, it was as snug as they could wish. After they had rested and Mustapha had changed into fresh robes, they went to dine.

The meal was hot and fortifying, rich soups and roasts served on beds of rice and barley, washed down with mulled wine and mead.

"Now," said Ayree, after the servants had cleared away the dishes, "to your problem."

"Noble lord," Mustapha replied, "I love this dog. He is all the family I have. Think of how I shall feel if one night, in his human shape, he is caught for stealing and hanged!"

"Why, then he has only to change back into a dog and baffle his would-be executioners," laughed the young sorcerer.

"But, Excellency, what if a householder should awaken to find the boy robbing him? The man does not call for the nightwatchmen but draws a sword or takes down a longbow and slays the intruder himself! Or what if, in the marketplace, the boy is caught with his hand in the pocket of his neighbor and his neighbor is a short-tempered soldier? Out comes the sword and off comes the boy's head before he can even think of changing back into his normal shape! There are even—forgive me, lord—some men who would burn my poor friend for being a witch if they so much as suspected his powers. The people of the Kestrel Mountains look dimly upon sorcery. Alas, there are many ignorant creatures in this world! What should I do then?"

The cloud of thought was upon Ayree's brow. Eight of his sisters, moved by Mustapha's plea, wept. Even Elcoloq began to whimper, imagining his own ignoble death. Ayree stood up and left his place at the table, still thinking. Suddenly he was not there. There was no flash, no noise, no puff of smoke, but the handsome young enchanter was gone all the same.

The oldest of Ayree's sisters gently touched Mustapha on the shoulder and said, "It is his way to vanish thus to a secret place when he would be alone to consider important things. He will help you, but he does not yet know how to do it. He shall return tomorrow. In the meantime go to your chamber and rest, and we shall entertain you this evening if you like."

Mustapha thanked her. Guided by one of the servants, he returned to his room, Elcoloq at his heels.

Chapter VI

DOG TIRED

Sun lit up the gelid walls of Mustapha's chamber, gently waking him. Elcoloq was already waiting for his master at the foot of the bed.

"Basoni said you were to pull the bell cord when you wanted breakfast," the dog said. "She's the one you saved, the littlest one, and she's very excited about being chosen to serve you."

"*You* saved us both, Elcoloq." Mustapha smiled. "I am no hero and I have no place in a hero's adventures. You ought to turn yourself human for good and take up the lost sword of Paragore-Tren, for you are more heroic than I."

"Modesty," mocked Elcoloq. "Are you so deluded as to believe that heroes are born to their adventures? They find them when they least seek them. They are the playthings of chance, just as you and I are. The fact remains, you killed the snow-beast and saved the child. Ring for her and let us have breakfast without further delay."

Mustapha nodded and pulled the cord. Immediately he heard the patter of small feet in the corridor and then Basoni was there, her long blond tresses caught up in plaits that crisscrossed atop her head. She bore a silver tray with a fine breakfast, including a bowl of meat and vegetables for the dog.

"My lord brother says he will speak with you after breakfast in the great hall, if that is pleasing to you, and I am to take him your answer," she said, as if reciting lessons. Her solemn little face dissolved into helpless giggles when she saw the curious look that Elcoloq gave her. "Oh, dear," she

41

sighed. "He's made me laugh, and I must be elegant because I still have to thank you for saving me. My brother said I shouldn't have run away, but I was so scared, and that ugly demon had kept me in her lodge for over a day when you came by. I'll start over." She cleared her throat and folded her hands formally before her. "Noble sir, my thanks for my life. I am yours to command." Elcoloq howled and the child giggled anew. "He doesn't know it's me with all the big-folk words," she explained to Mustapha.

"Neither do I," he teased. "Come, share breakfast with us. It is I who am yours to command, most magnificent of all royal ladies." He offered her the golden cakes on his tray, of which she gladly partook. It was altogether a festive romp of a breakfast.

Mustapha dressed quickly after Basoni left. He found the twelve sisters gathered in the great hall, seated at various tasks of needlework, study, or music making. Ayree sat at the far end of the hall on a long bench, playing with Basoni and her dolls. When he saw Mustapha, he sent his smallest sister off to play by herself and beckoned to the man and the dog.

"I fear," he said, "that I have news for you that will not be to your liking. I cannot disenchant your dog." Seeing the disappointment in Mustapha's face, Ayree explained: "When that particular spell of self-transformation was laid, there were a score of other spells flying about in the same small space at the same time. The casting of spells is a simple matter. Even my dearest little sister, Basoni, has learned to cast spells. Nay, even mortals cast them, unwittingly, from time to time.

"The skill of a sorcerer is not measured in what he can bewitch, but in what bewitchments he can undo. I speak not in self-praise when I say that I am one of the princes among sorcerers. Not only my ability at enchantments, but my knowledge of how to lift them, is almost without equal in the lands of the north and south. I can even cure those bewitched by wizards other than myself, or lift only part of an enchantment and leave the rest without harm. But Elcoloq has interwoven in him the spells of countless mages, until I am afraid that if I cure him of one spell, I shall have to cure him of all."

"Well, do it!" yapped Elcoloq. "Now I've a good master to serve, what care I if I speak or not?"

"Elcoloq, I had rather spend my time talking to myself and lose your valued conversation if it means your safety," said Mustapha.

Ayree shook his head sadly. "It is not that easy. This animal is so shot through with magics that I dare not try a thing. To lift one spell means to lift all, and to lift all might mean his death. I believe that enchantments weave together the pup's very existence. He might vanish from our sight, he might be hideously deformed, he might die!"

Mustapha hung his head. "Then there is no hope," he said dully.

Ayree touched him and spoke compassionately. "No hope to be had from me, you mean. There is always help to be sought elsewhere. You may even laugh when I tell you where!" But the look of pity in Ayree's eyes told Mustapha that he would not laugh at all.

"Yes, my lord Ayree?" he asked.

"You have traveled—much, I believe—and have associated with the usual people of the road: tumblers, jugglers, actors, bards. Your land of Vair is famous for its bards, I hear."

"Nay, Lord Ayree, we have the storytellers of the marketplace, but not bards such as in the northern lands."

"Yes, yes, I mean storytellers. And in their stories, perhaps you heard of the lands that lie to the south of Vair?"

"South of Vair!" Mustapha gasped. "You do not mean the lands of the Older Empire?"

"Yes, if that is their name. In the olden time there dwelt there a queen of such surpassing beauty and wisdom that she called the stars themselves from heaven to be her handmaidens, since the daughters of men were not fair enough to serve her."

"Nahrit!" barked Elcoloq. "Nahrit! The beautiful, the wise, the good, the gracious Queen Nahrit! 'Dead, dead, dead as the passing years is Queen Nahrit, and with her death the goodness of the world died, too. Men are made dogs, and dogs howl at the moon for empty pleasures, since that fairest of the daughters of the sun passed away. Weep, howl and weep, for she is gone; the dark river takes her.

And shall you dream, proud man, that it shall spare you?'"

The sisters of Ayree, hearing such a forceful recitation of Ruvida's immortal *Dirge for Queen Nahrit,* began to weep. Always the performer, Elcoloq took a bow and was about to proceed to the next stanza when Ayree interrupted.

"Not dead," said Ayree, "but living. Queen Nahrit is alive."

"Impossible!" Mustapha cried. "She was a daughter of the sun, a princess and queen of the Older Empire, and that has vanished from the earth for a thousand times a thousand years. Only ruins of the royal capital remain, and these are said to be accursed. None venture to view them. They lie far beyond the mountains of Vair, between the Desert of Thulain and the Lands of Wonder, where unknown beings dwell. Not even the desert hordes of Lord Olian dare go there, though they would ordinarily seek out the rich ruin to plunder it for the treasures of imperial tombs. The royal city lies deserted and untouched for these thousand thousand years, so how may Queen Nahrit still be alive?"

"Is it really that long?" asked Ayree. "A thousand thousand years?"

"It is but the way my people speak of a thing so lost in time that none can truly recall how old it is," said Mustapha. "Yet I think it is in this case a fair guess as to the age of Queen Nahrit, were she still alive."

"She is alive," Ayree insisted. "Last evening, when I left you, I retired to a place known only to myself, and from that place I sent out my call. I called to the Wise Ones to ask for some knowledge to show me how to lift the spell that rests on Elcoloq without harming him. Long did I call, and long I waited for an answer, peering into the night of my own making.

"No answer came. I was on the point of losing hope when there came to me in the blackness of my watching the face of a beautiful woman. She was crowned with a diadem of gold set with tiger's-eye, and her face also was golden, with the great, gilded eyes of a cat and thick waves of tawny hair. Regally robed was she in silks the color of the sunlit sea and as light as moondust. Her lips were red, as are the lips of many mortal women, but then she spoke in a voice so sweet it could only belong to a daughter of angels. And this vision said, 'Why do you call me? Queen Nahrit awaits.'

"I spoke, when the reverence I felt for such beauty allowed me to speak, and told her of your search. I told her that for unknown centuries men had spoken of the knowledge of Queen Nahrit, of her skill in wondrous sorceries. Then I asked her if she would help you."

"And will she?" Elcoloq asked, sitting up eagerly.

Ayree sighed. "The lady, the angel, the living breath of beauty did not answer me. She gazed and sighed as if her heart were bleeding away within her, but she would not answer. Then the vision was gone. I do not know what it means."

"Perhaps she shall speak to you again?" suggested Elcoloq hopefully.

"I have tried," said Ayree. "I have called to her. She does not answer. I fear she will never answer me."

Elcoloq pointed his muzzle at the ceiling and howled. It reverberated from the frozen rafters and echoed the length of the hall. "Woe!" cried the dog. "Woe for my master, woe for me!"

"Do not mourn, my friend," said Mustapha briskly. "We have no need for mourning when your help is almost in sight. If the lady Queen Nahrit yet lives and if she has the wisdom that may cure you, is that not half the struggle?"

"Ay-ay-ay-ay-yoooooooo! But she will not tell of it! She will not come to aid a miserable dog! She may be the prisoner of some evil spirits and cannot help me. Ay-yoooo!"

"Peace!" commanded Mustapha, and Elcoloq stopped in mid-howl. "She lives; that is all that is important. If she will not or cannot come to us, we shall go to her. If she be the prisoner of any spirit, we shall set her free that you may be healed. It is simple."

"But where are we to find her?" asked the dog.

"In my vision," said Ayree, "I beheld a great hall, carved all of huge blocks of yellow stone and pillared with jade. On the walls hung paintings such as I have never seen in this world. I have seen pitiful, crabbed imitations of such majestic murals as done by ancient scholars who say they are created in the style of the Older Empire. Only one place on earth could shelter such paintings, such pillars, and such a queen."

"Aye," said Mustapha. "The ruins of the Older Empire beyond the southern mountains of Vair." He seized Ayree's hands. "For your help and hospitality we cannot repay you, but we shall help you if we ever can. Now we must leave and venture southward, the sooner the better. You know our reasons."

Ayree patted Mustapha on the back. "Do not speak of repayment," he said. "I wish you a safe journey and pray to be reunited with you again someday. My sisters will prepare your things for the trip. Do not reject my parting gifts to you. Farewell."

Leaving the hall, man and dog returned to Mustapha's room, where they found all of their effects packed in leather saddlebags. New robes were provided for Mustapha and a fine purse of money besides.

"How could they do all this so swiftly?" the man wondered.

"Master, you forget that they are sisters of the warlock prince. Their powers are small as yet, but one day I predict we shall hear more of the twelve sisters of Ayree," said Elcoloq.

They were conducted to the gate of Castle Snowglimmer, where a silvery steed was saddled and waiting. Ayree's eldest sister held the bridle and said, "It is our brother's horse. He can but lend it to you. It will bear you as far south as the first true town, where Ayree requests that you dismount, turn the horse's nose to the north, and send him on his way."

Mustapha promised to comply. There were tears and goodbye kisses, more for Elcoloq from the smaller sisters, and then in a spray of powdery snow the wanderers galloped away to the south.

From the battlements of Castle Snowglimmer, Ayree watched them. He felt a curl of warm breath in his ear and saw that the eldest of his sisters had joined him.

"You might have gone with them," she said. "Your powers could have taken them to the very court of Queen Nahrit in an instant."

Ayree shook his head. "You do not understand all of magic yet, my sister. The world is older than magic, but not so old as prophecy."

"Prophecy!" The maiden laughed. "Are you dwelling on that foolish scroll again? How can a lost book have any power for more than gathering dust? And from what you have told me of it, the scroll is no collection of magic spells, but only the tale of a dead hero. Mere fiction! Let the scroll stay lost, then, if it worries you so."

"You will come to remember those words," said Ayree, "perhaps with regret. The lost scroll shall save us if we find it; and the fate of the Twelve Kingdoms is hidden in it. If it is destroyed, if it falls into evil hands, we are lost. A hero must find and return it to the realm of light."

Ayree's sister laughed again. "Well, that one with his talking dog didn't look like a hero to me. I know the prophecy: 'A hero walks alone.' But he knows nothing of heroics or quests or grand deeds and battles, that Mustapha. He is only a homeless wanderer with a kindly heart."

Ayree said nothing, turning his eyes to the vanishing dot that was Mustapha and his wise dog riding together on the silver steed into the southlands. Truly, his sister was still very young, he thought, to know so little of heroes.

Chapter VII

DOGGEREL

Of Mustapha's return to the southern lands few tales are told. Many assume that he and Elcoloq proceeded on foot after returning Ayree's horse to the north. When their coins were gone they went back to performing for their supper, following any hint they might hear of a noble seeking entertainers for a festival in his castle. Usually they roamed the roads alone, though sometimes they took up with others of their craft and toured the Twelve Kingdoms as part of an ensemble.

One such troupe was Polkin's Polyphonic Players, and this was the manner of their meeting.

Mustapha's poor finances made the trip south a very indirect, zigzag journey, as they were always taken out of their way by news of a town fair or a royal feast where they might find employment. It so happened that the wanderers found themselves in the kingdom of Heydista, where King Cranshaw the Crabbed ruled. But the rumor of the marriage of King Cranshaw to a princess of Glytch had been merely a rumor. Heydista, once as merry a land as any other, had become somber and staid under Cranshaw's sober rule. With good reason Mustapha and Elcoloq feared that this kingdom would not hold many fairs or festivals at which to make a living.

They sat beside the road and wondered what to do. They had already played out the surrounding lands. In the midst of pondering where next to try their luck, they heard music, like the music children make on washtubs and combs when they play at being wandering minstrels. The players came in sight, and Mustapha and his dog saw that they were not children at all, though in fact they were playing on combs and washtubs.

First came a thin, sallow-faced young man dressed in an elaborately ragged tunic of yellow silk. You could tell where he had been and what he had eaten by the stains on it. Thus wearing his autobiography, he marched ahead of the others, carrying a white banner emblazoned with a gold phoenix.

After him came the musicians. They looked like twins, both clad in torn white hose and tattered brown velvet coats. A short though majestic blond man strode behind them, wearing a shirt of white linen that was turning lemony with age, a long tunic of parti-colored satin coming apart at the seams, hose so old that Mustapha couldn't guess their original color, and shoes whose rusty leather was beginning to crack.

By the hand this man led a lovely woman whose golden hair rivaled the curls of Ayree's sisters in hue and profusion. Just as her escort was the worst-clad fellow Mustapha had ever seen, so was she the most sumptuously turned-out person of all that ragtag company. Her gown was of the finest satin, tinted like a budding rose, all trimmed with snowflake lace at throat and cuffs. A fillet of this same lace bound her magnificent hair. So full-skirted was her gown that one could only briefly glimpse the tiny golden slippers she wore upon her dainty feet.

Elcoloq bounded straight for the fair lady, stopped smack in the middle of her path, and barked loudly. He sat up for her, wagging his tail, yet in all his outburst of affection he took care not to lay a paw on her gorgeous clothes. The lady was pleased with this display, for she laughed and tried to catch the dog up in her arms. This Elcoloq allowed her to do, though he still made every effort to keep his dirty paws away from her satin gown.

"Oh, what an adorable puppy!" sighed the lady. By no wild imaginings could Elcoloq be called a puppy! "Is he yours?"

"Fairest Flower of the Garden of the World," said Mustapha, slipping easily back into the gallant, flowery speech of the south, "this unworthy beast is indeed mine. Yet even the dumb beasts of the earth know that they must pay homage to such beauty as is yours."

"My wife thanks you," the man in the parti-colored tunic said tersely.

Mustapha now turned to him and made an elaborate bow. "I stand in awe and reverence before one whom the gods must love exceeding well. I am Mustapha; if I may serve you in any way, though I am nothing more than a simple animal trainer and wandering player, I hope you will allow me to do so."

The lady, whose name was Gatica, begged her husband to let them join the troupe. Polkin did not need much persuading. He was a nice fellow, good-humored and wise—though of a biting wit when crossed—and he saw the good sense of hiring an itinerant animal act to warm up the audience before a play. Elcoloq performed and Polkin was convinced. They were hired.

Life with Polkin's Polyphonic Players was more diverting for Mustapha than for Elcoloq. The poor dog had to conceal his gift of speech lest someone should think to steal and sell him. Only at night in their own tent could Mustapha and his dog converse, and then only in whispers. They agreed that in spite of the inconvenience to Elcoloq, life with the troupe was better than roaming the roads alone.

"I don't mind having to keep quiet," the dog hissed. "At least we're eating regularly."

"Security is a small price to pay for your silence," agreed Mustapha. "They are good people and good friends to us already. I have had even better news for Polkin today than I ever hoped for. The Polyphonic Players will travel south, then cross the Opalza Sea to tour the southern lands."

"Remarkable, master! Our fortune has changed."

"Well," Mustapha said modestly, "I did happen to drop a hint or two in Polkin's ear about the great bazaar of Ishma and the generosity of the audiences in Vair."

In their travels Elcoloq became attached to Gatica, Polkin's wife and the prima donna of the company. The only other actress among them was Marfisa, Gatica's maiden aunt. The older woman had raised Gatica and had once been a prima donna herself. Now she played more mature roles. Between aunt and niece, Elcoloq had ribbons tied around his neck, soft pillows to sleep on, constant brushings, scented fur, and plenty of bonbons to eat. He reveled in it.

Polkin's Polyphonic Players did not have a very large

repertoire, but Polkin was proud to say that the few they could perform were classics: *The Anonymous Sausage-Maker, The Tragedy of a Night's Necessity, Perdix and Perdita,* and *The Revels of Recared.* Besides Polkin, Gatica, and Marfisa, the company included Maigrus, the sallow man who bore the troupe's banner; Mingo and Revulgo, the twin musicians; Harfort, who played male romantic leads when Polkin was indisposed; and Bretswin, an older actor who took fatherly roles and for whom Marfisa nourished a chaste passion.

The company was well received almost everywhere. True, there were a few incidents that caused them to leave a village or two earlier than planned. For the most part Gatica caused these accidents of fortune—though certainly not deliberately. Her great beauty would inflame the senses of some bumpkin, and if the bumpkin's father happened to be influential in the town, difficulties would arise. To avoid such encounters, Polkin led his players on to the next village before things could get out of hand. To the everlasting sorrow of Mustapha and Elcoloq, there came a day when Polkin was not able to avoid the conflict.

Polkin's Polyphonic Players, like any other actors, were always glad of a summons to play before nobility. A summons of this kind came one day from the ducal castle of Glytch. Glytch lies upon the Opalza Sea, and Polkin thought to take ship from there to Malbenu Isle as soon as they had enough for passage; from Malbenu they would proceed to Vair. But the entire voyage depended on earning enough in Glytch to afford tickets for them all—their one hope being to perform for some rich patron. Now they had that opportunity.

Duke Emtrans of Glytch was exceptionally wealthy. He was furthermore exceptional in that he did not abuse his wealth. He might have bought and sold the king and the kingdom of Glytch with his riches; instead he gave his days over to study and good works. His face radiated kindness and peace.

Family matters were the only thing that troubled him. The players heard much of Duke Emtrans' sorrows when they stopped for the night at the Pork Tree Inn, a day's journey northwest of the duke's castle.

The innkeeper of the Pork Tree was a guarded man whose attempts at playing the jovial host were sporadic and absurd.

He preferred gossip to trading rough jokes with the patrons. Fortunately for his business, his wife tended the bar, telling rude stories with the bluff relish of an old soldier, and leaving the innkeeper to indulge his taste for telling long tales about the nobility of Glytch. He ended each story with the morose prediction that no good would come of it.

"Duke Emtrans, he's a fine fellow," said the host as he served the players their beer. "His wife's a good soul, too, daughter of a poor knight. Well, folks around here said that no good would come of that marriage. He married her for her goodness, not her fortune, and they've been happy for years."

"How sweet!" exclaimed Gatica, clapping her hands. "Maigrus, you must write a play about this at once. How romantic it all is—the good duke, the poor knight's daughter, the happy ending. It's just like us, my love," she remarked to Polkin. "Didn't I leave my chance to wed a wealthy suitor because my heart was yours?"

The innkeeper shook his head and refilled their mugs with foamy brew. "No good *has* come of it," he intoned. "They live in harmony and she has given him three sons and two daughters, but there is a cloud above them that waits for the moment to unleash a thunderbolt on their heads."

"Get away with you, gore-crow!" shouted the innkeeper's wife, giving her mate a hearty shove away from the table. "My man's a croaker," she explained. "The good duke and his dear duchess live happily with their children. The older daughter has married, and now the younger one takes a husband. You look like players. Do you go to the castle for the entertainments?"

Polkin allowed as they did.

"Well, when you get there you will see that this old glumface is full of suds. Two daughters like two roses! And as for the sons, they are all—"

"Ah, no, wife!" The innkeeper's sonorous voice tolled through her words of praise. "They are *not* all."

"They are all good young men," the wife maintained, turning on her husband. "You believe the evil rumors about the duke's second son all you like. I'll go to my grave swearing that it's all falsehood. He's a brisk young man and still feeling his oats; that's all that ails him."

The innkeeper shook his head slowly, like a bullock. "It

is more than that," he said. "More than that. No good will
come of it, mark my words. Enjoy your meal, noble patrons."

The following morning took them to Duke Emtrans' castle. It was so large that the duke was able to offer guest
rooms to the multitude of players who had come to perform
at the wedding festivities. Polkin's Polyphonic Players received two large rooms to themselves and part of their fee
in advance. When they got the entire sum it would be plenty
to take them to Malbenu Isle, with cash left over.

"We ought to perform *The Anonymous Sausage-Maker*
for the wedding," said Polkin. "True love triumphant and
all that. Most appropriate."

"Remember Wister, the stern father," Gatica objected.
"He might offend Duke Emtrans. I prefer *Perdix and Perdita*. The true love is just as triumphant there and the father
is nicer."

"My dear," Polkin replied, "while I admit that *Perdix
and Perdita* lives among the immortal works of drama, I
don't think a play in which the entire cast dies is the thing
to perform at a wedding. Call me conservative if you like."

On the day before the marriage they were given a hall
in which to rehearse. Mustapha and Elcoloq retired to a
corner to practice their new routines of tricks while the actors
ran through the play. Elcoloq had a little trouble with his
new dance and Gatica did no better with some of her lines,
so while the others went off to take refreshment, Mustapha,
Elcoloq, and Gatica had the hall to themselves.

"Dear Mustapha," Gatica said, "would you mind setting
up these folding partitions and rehearsing behind them. I'm
having so much trouble with this speech, and I can't con-
centrate with you here. Every time I look at Elcoloq, I laugh.
It's not very dramatic."

Mustapha bowed with southern grace. "Personification
of the Goddess Ambra," he said, "we obey."

He tugged the screens into place and then took Elcoloq
out of sight behind them. The only sound in the hall was
Gatica's sweet voice repeating the troublesome lines in different intonations to see which one suited her best. The
impassioned actress's voice muffled the scratch of Elcoloq's
claws on the flagstone floor. Elcoloq had just begun to get
the dance right when he paused in mid-step. There was the

sound of the hall door being opened and the clash of mail-clad feet striding across the stones.

"Please go on," said a cold, wicked voice. "You are most beautiful when you act—nay, most beautiful always, even with the dust of travel upon you. When you came into the courtyard of my father's castle, I thought you lovely. You are a thousand times mo: : lovely now."

"My lord," Gatica chided. "Such talk is unseemly. I am a married woman."

"And a very young one. Is your husband so young?"

"No older than I, if it concerns you."

"And yet," the voice went on, "things may happen even to young men."

"What things do you speak of?" Gatica demanded, her voice shrill with apprehension.

"Nay, lady, I jest, I jest. Will you give me a kiss for putting your mind to rest?" The sound of armored feet was heard again, coming closer to where Gatica stood, then a scrape of wood on stone and a little huff of effort from the lady.

"Stand back or I'll kiss you with this chair!" she said. Peering through a crack in the partition, Mustapha saw Gatica, a sturdy chair held above her head, facing a young man of aristocratic appearance. Mustapha recognized him as the duke's second son, presented in the general introductory audience with the noble family.

"Put down the chair," commanded the man, with the calm of black waters. "Such behavior is improper for a duchess."

"You have seen me play the part, or perhaps you wish to lure me to your arms with wicked promises. I am no duchess, but if you come any closer I'll crown you king!"

The fellow laughed. "You have hit it, my lady! It is a promise I've often used on brainless country wenches. Your mind equals your beauty. To you I make the offer of a ducal crown sincerely. Would you not prefer to be a duchess in truth, and not just in a play that lasts for a few moments upon a ramshackle stage? I am the duke's well-beloved son Tor and shall one day be duke myself, my lady wife the duchess."

"Good fortune to her, then," retorted Gatica. "You nourish pretty dreams. You have an elder brother and he shall be the duke, in any case."

"Brothers"—Tor grinned—"are transient things."

Gatica gasped, catching his terrible meaning. "You would not—not do this thing?"

"To make you a duchess, my lady, I'd do more. For I do think you are encumbered with a husband unworthy of your beauty and grace. Fortunately, husbands are no more durable or lasting than brothers."

"Nay, stay back! You shall not do this thing! Not while I live!"

Mustapha peeked through the crevice and saw Gatica hurl the chair at Tor with an unsuspected strength; then she fled the room as he ducked it. The duke's son pursued her, leaving Mustapha and Elcoloq alone in the hall.

"I mislike this," Mustapha said.

"So do I," Elcoloq agreed.

"We must tell Polkin, and quickly."

"Right, master. Do it at once, with wings," suggested the dog.

Polkin only laughed when Mustapha told him what he had seen. "A young man's fancy!" Polkin exclaimed. "Such is always Gatica's fate. She knows how to handle them; Tor is but one of many."

"He means great evil," Mustapha urged. "He has the eyes of a man who'd as soon kill a king as a kipper."

"If this were as serious as you make it, gloomtroll, why has not Gatica come to me about it?"

"Because," said Gatica, entering the room, "I thought it best to put both the duke and his eldest son on their guard before telling you. Duke Emtrans does not take all this so lightly. And I was right to warn him: He has been perturbed by the actions of his second son for a long time. The boy was always darkly secretive. He turns aside from good, calling it the occupation of fools, and lately he has taken to associating with supramortal evils. Daily, Duke Emtrans hears reports that his son has been seen in the gatherings of wicked folk. They pay homage to the demons of the Naimlô Wood; and some even worship he who dwells beyond it." She dared not say the hated name.

"And what will the duke do?" asked Polkin.

"He watches. What more can he do, until Tor makes some first move of open evil? After all, it is his *son* we are speaking of. But the duke has rewarded me, so we may leave in safety now for the southern lands on the first boat out. I'll have Aunt Marfisa start the packing."

Gatica would have left the room, but Polkin cried, "Hold! The wedding is tomorrow. We cannot leave without giving our performance. It would be breach of contract."

"Will you not understand?" Gatica wailed. "This Tor is dangerous! Even his own father realizes it! I rebuffed him, and I betrayed him to his father; he will certainly seek to harm us. We *must* go! The duke will understand."

"The duke, perhaps, but not I," Polkin said calmly. "Our reputation will be worthless if it becomes known that we accepted payment for no performance. If the duke knows of Tor's plans, he cannot harm us. You worry too much. One more day here means nothing."

Having seen Tor's cold eyes, Mustapha did not share Polkin's complacency, but he did not think it was his place to correct his employer. Gatica begged and pleaded with her husband for a while, but Polkin's logical and soothing arguments eventually set her mind at ease, and she agreed to perform at the wedding.

"Have Marfisa pack our things if you like, dear," he told her. "We'll leave directly after the show; we can travel in our *Anonymous Sausage-Maker* costumes to save time. Here, I'll tell you what! Mustapha, you and your dog perform first, then go with this money"—Polkin tossed Mustapha the purse from the duke—"to the seaport. It is only a few hours' march from here. Purchase our passages. We'll meet you halfway between the castle and the docks as soon as we finish the play. 'Tis not far."

Mustapha took the money and bowed. "You place great trust in me," he said.

"Well placed, well placed," the placid Polkin assured him, slapping his back. "There, my love," the actor said to his wife. "Now are you content?"

Gatica said she was, but her expression told another story. Still, as Polkin seemed untroubled by any threats Tor might produce, she tried to cheer up for his sake. Being a good actress, she succeeded in convincing even herself that she had been quite foolish to worry.

Chapter VIII

DOGMATIC

Good Duke Emtrans did not look happy. Given the joyous occasion of his daughter's wedding, his sadness was odd. The courtiers noted it, but did not wonder at its cause, for they well knew the evil life that young Tor led. Still, they thought they had once seen some grain of hope in the duke's face when he gazed upon that strange son of his. Now his look held only pity and despair. The duke's men-at-arms kept watch on Tor, while a specially-picked contingent never for a minute left the side of the duke's eldest son.

Tor's own men-at-arms escorted him. They were of quite another cut from those who guarded Tor's elder brother. At Tor's request, the duke had let him recruit the ten armed followers of his personal suite. He did not select them from the lesser nobility, but rather seemed to have skimmed the scum of a dozen taverns and jails to come up with this wretched crew. They had been cleaned up and dressed well and taught manners aplenty to make them fit unobtrusively into the ducal household, yet there was still the odor of alleyway murderers about them, and the court gave them a wide berth.

The great hall where the wedding was fêted came to resemble two armed camps. Mustapha and his wise dog were sent out to warm up the audience before the main body of the entertainments.

"Ah, easily said," Mustapha whispered to Elcoloq. "It would take a bonfire to warm up this lot!"

Their act received polite applause. A few even tossed handfuls of gold to Mustapha after the performance. The gold pieces thrilled and thrummed in his hand with the tension of the room. He was very glad when at last he could leave with Elcoloq to book passage to Malbenu Isle.

The moon was full and the road to the seaport was clear, for the most part running fair through open fields. At one point a small patch of forest intercepted the road, much too insignificent for any band of cutthroats to use as an ambush. Nevertheless, Mustapha felt relieved when they left the shadows of the trees behind them.

A sturdy ship lay in the harbor, and by good luck it was leaving that night for Malbenu. The captain was a fine old sailor, honest of face and mien, who promised Mustapha and his friends a safe, if not luxurious, voyage. He asked to see the money, to make sure they could pay, but refused to accept it until they should all embark.

"I'm no fool," he explained. "I'll not have you cheat me. On the other hand, neither am I a cheat. I'll take no coin till you're well aboard, nor shall I leave without you. When come your companions?"

"They are still at the castle of Duke Emtrans," said Mustapha. "I go back now to meet them midway on the road."

"Midway from there to here? You haven't far to go, then. Come, have a bit of brandy with me to warm you against the night air!"

The captain took him aboard ship, into his private cabin. The brandy was Sombrunian, and in that land they brew their brandy strong to ward off the mists and damp from the sea. The captain's idea of "a bit" of brandy was an old sailor's estimate: He filled a horn half-full of the amber liquid and pressed Mustapha to drink it all. For Elcoloq, the captain found some ship's biscuit.

"Drink! Drink!" he encouraged Mustapha. "The nights here are deadly cold. Why, you sip like a lady! Here, drink like a man, my friend!" He filled his own horn to the brim and drained it at a gulp, then refilled it and repeated the operation.

Mustapha took heart from this display and swallowed his drink manfully. His eyes watered over, and he coughed as the brandy's subtle fires seared his insides. The captain knew of only one cure for that sort of coughing.

"Here, have another," he said, this time filling the horn and pouring it down Mustapha's throat. The coughing stopped, fried to a crisp. Mustapha had the look of a drunken chicken.

"Elcoloq," he murmured, slipping smoothly out of his chair to join his dog on the floor. "Elcoloq, this shall forever be my bes' frien' in all th' worl'. Cap'n, I'm y' hum'le scrvant. How say you, doggie?"

Mustapha's eyes closed and he beamed goodwill to all the universe. The captain chuckled and addressed the bemused dog.

"There's a new one for me, my buck! Some that taste Sombrunian brandy for the first time will think they're hemmed in by lovely maidens. Some will think they can fly. This is the first one who ever thought his dog could hear him, understand, and reply. Men grow foolish with drink!"

"Yes, don't they?" remarked Elcoloq.

"What did you say?" demanded the captain, feeling his knees turn watery.

"Woof," Elcoloq repeated, a look of pure innocence on his face. "Woof, woof, woof."

The captain shook his head and sighed. It must be true, he thought, that as one grew older one could not bear the effects of strong drink quite so well. He bent down to revive Mustapha before he imagined the dog would speak a second time.

"Here, friend, wake up! You must go and meet your companions on the road, you said."

Mustapha blinked and then sprang to his feet. The deck lurched beneath him, making him imagine that he had been kidnapped and taken to sea while sleeping. He peered out the porthole at the reassuring sight of the docks in the moonlight.

"You're right," he said, grinning sheepishly. "We must go. Come, Elcoloq." They left with the captain's good wishes.

The Sombrunian brandy still worked its charms inside Mustapha. The journey back toward the castle did not seem half so strenuous or tedious as the trip to the seaport. However, while the return trip was pleasant, it also seemed to pass more slowly.

"I am weary," Mustapha complained to the moon. "Why should I go all that way back again? They will find me here if they pass the halfway mark and keep on going; what matter if I rest my weary bones and take a bit of a nap? Elcoloq, you can keep watch and tell me if you see them coming, can't you?"

"Master," replied the sage animal, "you must have been sleeping when the gods granted wisdom. If you sprawl by the wayside out here in the open, any fool can come along and rob you, slitting your throat into the bargain. If sleep you must, at least conceal yourself. I will watch the road and wake you, as you say."

"O wise beast!" Mustapha sighed. "I hear and am counseled."

By this time the little patch of forest was in sight on the moon-drenched plain. Elcoloq nodded and advised Mustapha that this would indeed be a suitable place to rest unmolested.

"As for me, I shall go to the edge of the forest that lies nearer the castle, there to watch for the players," the dog said.

The moonlit forest beckoned the tired traveler with its beds of silvery-green moss made soft by blankets of pine needles. His pack for a pillow, Mustapha was soon fast asleep.

He was awakened by Elcoloq gently licking his ear. "Are they here?" he asked. The sleep had refreshed him wonderfully. He scrambled to his feet, ready to greet his friends, but Elcoloq restrained him. By the light of the moon that flooded the small wood with brilliant light, Mustapha saw the look of tragedy in Elcoloq's eyes. Dogs do not weep, not in our own manner, but they can mourn better than we, having no such easy outlet for their grief as tears. Now Mustapha saw that Elcoloq's very heart was being torn asunder and that his sorrow was so great and unspeakable a thing that he could not even howl.

"O Elcoloq, Prince of My Heart, speak!" he begged. "Tell me, why is there such sorrow in your face; what pain makes your heart such a burden unto you?" He hugged Elcoloq close and stroked his head until finally the dog let a piercing howl burst forth into the night.

"O my master, what have I seen? Why do I live to have seen such things?" wailed the dog. "Must I tell you what I have beheld? Must I show you, that you must likewise mourn? Nay, nay, ask me rather to die!"

"To show me? Then it lies nearby, this thing that has hurt you?" asked Mustapha, coldness enveloping his heart.

"Sit, my master, for I will tell you first. Then it may not be so shocking when you must see what I have seen." At Elcoloq's words, Mustapha sat and listened.

"I stood watch," began the dog, "as you bade me, searching the road from the castle for our friends. Soon I heard the welcome sounds of their voices, accompanied by the music they made so cheerily."

"Made?" repeated Mustapha, fearing much.

"Hush, let me speak," said the dog gently. "I heard them, but waited until I might see them. There is a slight dip, an infant hill that lies between the forest and the castle. They sounded close enough to be climbing it. Indeed, I saw the top of their banner and the gangling figure of Maigrus already at the summit. I even think he may have seen me, white as I am against the darker trees. And then . . . hoofbeats.

"At first I hoped the horses were theirs, a reward from good Duke Emtrans. My heart denied this, even as my mind suggested it. The horses were not theirs. Other travelers, I thought next, and then I was afraid. I suspected too well who came riding after them so swiftly, so coldly.

"They had no chance to flee, no real chance to defend themselves. Eleven men on horseback, all armed, against six unarmed men and two women. Polkin they slew first, swords gleaming in the moonlight. Mingo and Revulgo swiftly followed their master to cruel death. They were only boys! Maigrus tried to defend Marfisa and Gatica using the pole of his banner as a lance. They laughed before they cut his head off. Harfort had a prop sword of barely serviceable quality. What use was one sword when so many opposed him? He died, but with the satisfaction of taking one of them with him. Even old Bretswin tried to protect the women, yet the riders showed no respect for his years. That was their mistake. The old man took up Harfort's sword and cut down two before they in turn slew him.

"Gatica saw at once who had slain her husband and her friends. She knew she was not meant to die. Proud and black as an iron statue, Tor sat his stallion against the hunter's moon and spoke to her with mocking courtesy.

"'See, my lady,' he said, prancing up to her. 'See how

truly I spoke when I said that husbands were transitory things. Let this teach you to believe my words in future. Take her!' he barked to his men. 'Take her alive and bring her with us. She scorned to be my duchess, so she shall act another part for me. For all of you as well, when I tire of her!'

"Gatica wore an ornamental dagger at her belt and drew it, slashing at Tor's horse. The steed reared and danced away while Tor's men dismounted to capture her. She menaced them with the blade as they drew nearer. How the jackals laughed! They thought to easily disarm her. One seized her old aunt, Marfisa, and said he would kill her if Gatica did not surrender. Tor dismounted and held the knife to the old woman's throat; Gatica hesitated.

"Then—O noble woman!—Marfisa lunged forward, falling on the knife. Her niece beheld the old lady's valor and stood firm on her guard. The hunters circled her where she stood, tightening the noose. She let them approach. Then, when they were near enough, she charged through their circle, slashing two of them grievously. At last she stood above the body of her slain husband—I could not see her eyes to tell if sorrow had driven her mad or if it was courage alone that made her turn the dagger against her own breast and die there, upon the shimmering plain."

Finished, Elcoloq hung his head. Mustapha asked harshly, "And those that slew them? Where are they, who killed my friends while I slept? Why did you not fetch me to aid them?"

"Alas, master! What could you have done but die with them? The enemy was too great, too many. After, I drew closer on my belly through the roadside weeds to hear what the butchers would say. Tor bade his henchmen carry away their carrion brethren for burial, but to leave the bodies of our friends where they had fallen. They loaded their horses with their dead and galloped off. Then I saw Tor wheel his horse away and ride into the west. May it be the direction of his doom!"

Mustapha patted Elcoloq tenderly. "You did well," he said. "I could not have saved them, but now I can do them a last service."

He looked up to where the lights of a farmhouse shone faintly across the fields. He weighed the purse of gold that was to have borne him and his friends to freedom.

"Here, Elcoloq," he said, tying a portion of the gold into a kerchief and fastening it around the dog's neck. "Go to the port, to the captain. I'll write you a note to take him. . . . There! 'Tis written." Mustapha attached the note to the kerchief. "Meanwhile I shall go to yonder house and hire the use of a spade with what is left of the money. I shall bury them, Elcoloq. That is all I may do for them in this life."

"But, master," protested Elcoloq, "are we not to keep some gold to pay our own passage to Malbenu?"

"This gold is not ours, but theirs. I shall set aside our wages from it, and no more. If we kept the purse and went to Malbenu, the gold would curse us and keep us there forever. The living are powerful, but not so powerful as the dead. We shall use the gold we earn ourselves to reach the court of Queen Nahrit or we won't go at all."

Elcoloq nodded, then raced down the shining road, while Mustapha trudged across the shadowy fields on his own unhappy mission.

Chapter IX

THE DOGS OF SPRING

For a time after that sad night, Mustapha nourished hopes of vengeance; but the second son of Duke Emtrans vanished from Glytch, and no one knew where he had gone. Years later, after all such thoughts had faded to dim longing, Mustapha had the fortune to watch this same villain meeting a suitably painful end. But that is another story.

Mustapha and Elcoloq went back to performing. Never again did they join a troupe, for doing so would have stirred up memories of their former happiness with Polkin's Polyphonic Players, and of their loss. The two passed through years of wandering, seeing the changes that washed across the Twelve Kingdoms. At last Mustapha and Elcoloq found themselves upon the shores of the southern lands.

They were in Sombrunia, famous for heroes and brandy; a goodly country that lies far to the west of the southern lands. Though its customs and costumes seem more akin to those of the northern lands, it is a southern land all the same.

In his travels Mustapha always wore the flowing robes of his native Vair. This peculiar mode of dress drew attention to him in the northern cities; it helped business. In Sombrunia, for the first time since he had left Vair to go north, Mustapha again saw men robed as he was—with certain minor variations. The Sombrunian nobles and royal court wore northern-style clothes, but among the common folk there was a mix of costumes.

The capital of Sombrunia boasted a fine port that lured in the merchant ships of Vair, while from across the nearby Desert of Thulain came the caravans of Lord Olian's people.

Many of the southern races made a temporary home in Sombrunia, and some made permanent settlements there, for the ruler of Sombrunia was more benevolent and less demanding than the Council of Vair or the dread Lord Olian. The southerners came, and they brought their manners and dress with them.

Mustapha repaired to the main bazaar of the capital as soon as he could, to earn some cash by Elcoloq's tricks. The dog had not relapsed into his old vice of transformation since the death of Polkin's troupe. In truth, he had changed his form once—but for battle, not petty theft. (But that's another tale.) Nevertheless, Mustapha felt it was his duty to forbid Elcoloq to even think of turning human while they were in Sombrunia.

"We have money and a place at the Inn of the Camel Drivers for tonight. We shall have a hearty dinner and a few coins left over besides. So none of your shenanigans; is that clear?"

"But, master," Elcoloq insinuated winningly, "and tomorrow? Must we worry about tomorrow when I might so easily bring us a purse—a small, an insignificant purse!— that would support us for a few more days? This is a busy city, master. No one will notice me if—"

"Enough! None of that. I vow, you seem to miss your old occupation, Elcoloq. But you shall not resume it. You are out of practice and could be caught, so put such thoughts aside. The sooner we find your cure, the calmer I'll sleep."

The mention of sleep made Elcoloq yawn; and there is nothing more contagious than a dog's long, narrow, pink yawn. "Let us sleep on it, master," Elcoloq decided, leading the way from the bazaar to the Inn of the Camel Drivers.

True to its name, the inn already had several camel drivers in the taproom, drinking. They greeted Mustapha, seeing by his dress that he was southern-born like themselves. "And not," as one of them snarled, "one of these transplanted northern swine that rule Sombrunia!"

"But, O Son of a Philosopher," interposed Mustapha, "what do you have against the legal rulers of this land?"

Though the man was half drunk, he knew when he had been insulted. "Because, Child of a Night Watchman, this land might otherwise belong to us southern folk, who can better use it."

"Why argue, brethren?" a kindly older driver asked, seeking to prevent a quarrel. "We of the southern lands would not enjoy Sombrunia. It is too like the north for us. Better we remain in the golden warmth of the desert or the cool glory of the mountains and leave Sombrunia to men who appreciate fogs, snow, and hail. The gods had reasons when they set Sombrunia apart from the other southern lands, using two mountain ranges and the Dunenfels Plain! Do not question the wisdom of the gods."

Having confused the drunk enough to forestall a fight, the older man retired to his corner and again took up the mouthpiece of his chibouk. Mustapha, followed by Elcoloq, joined him in silence at the low table.

"My thanks, graybeard," said Mustapha. "I dislike a quarrel as much as the next man, but that toad came near to provoking me. I have great love for the true rulers of Sombrunia."

"As do I, my son, as do I." The old man chuckled, reflectively smoothing his scraggly beard.

"You have the air, graybeard, of one who is much traveled," Mustapha said tentatively, for he nourished hope of getting cheap passage eastward to Vair with this pleasant old soul.

"Aye," said the man. "I am a camel driver, a caravan guide, as are most of us here. Yet you, my son, have not the air of the camel driver about you." Here he laughed and pinched his nostrils in the common joke.

"With the help of my dog, I am a performer," said Mustapha. "I do not find as much business as I'd like in Sombrunia. I hope to travel to Vair, there to earn my livelihood at the great bazaar of Ishma. He who cannot earn enough upon which to live at the great bazaar of Ishma must be marked by the gods to perish of starvation in this life."

"Let us call upon the gods of coincidence, my son, and render thanks to them. In all honesty, I am bound for Vair tomorrow. If you and your dog are good players, you can earn places in my caravan by entertaining myself and the other drivers."

"Support of orphans!" Mustapha cried joyously, clasping the old man's hand in his. "We will show you now how well we shall entertain you all!" He made as if to begin Elcoloq's act, but the old man detained him.

"No, my son, it is not needful. We shall see on the road. I trust you well. Until tomorrow at dawn." He got slowly to his feet and retired to his room. Mustapha had a thimbleful of brandy to celebrate his good luck, and gave a taste of the strong spirit to Elcoloq, who promptly sneezed. Then they too retired.

Dawn came cold and misty in Sombrunia, but the courtyard of the Inn of the Camel Drivers was already warm with the breath of men and beasts. The camels moaned and grunted, spitting and biting at anyone within reach, but somehow they were loaded and harnessed. Saddles creaked and bells jingled as the tall, knob-kneed animals lurched to their feet. The old man who had offered Mustapha passage to Vair with the caravan was giving orders from his throne upon a worn-out camel saddle set on a mounting block. There Mustapha found him and knelt before him.

"Good! You seem a willing traveler, my son." The old man smiled. "Since we must travel far together, by what name is your most excellent self known?"

"I am Mustapha the Orphan," replied Mustapha, using the common formula for those who did not wish to reveal their family name.

"And I," said his friend, "am Nailuj, son of Pelegavo—though my father is no more, so I suppose you might call me Nailuj the Orphan, too!" He laughed and patted Mustapha on the back. "Are you ready to leave?"

"Yes, Help of the Oppressed," replied Mustapha, showing his small pack of belongings.

"Excellent. You shall ride in my own palanquin," said Nailuj, leading him to where a single pure-white camel stood like a mountain of snow against the dawning sky. Mustapha had never seen such a magnificent specimen, nor such an expensive and exquisite harness. It was all of scarlet leather with silver hardware and glass bells. The palanquin was smaller than the kind used by women, but it was every bit as comfortable, being shaded from the sun, curtained against sudden sandstorms, and cushioned to offset bumpy roads.

Who can describe a journey on camelback? After the first days of pitching and swaying, with stops too infrequent for true comfort, one becomes accustomed to it. Mustapha had often ridden on such animals and found this part of his trip rather tedious. East went the caravan from the capital of Sombrunia, where stands Castle Pibroch. They reached the first mountain range and crossed without incident. This brought them to the wide wastes of the Dunenfels Plain.

If land can be gray, then the Dunenfels Plain is that sorry color; yet the eye protests it cannot be so. Grass grows in abundance there, and surely grass cannot be gray? Wild horses and sheep graze together with smaller creatures and seem to enjoy that grass, no matter what color it appears to men. Wild creatures thrive and fatten on it, but the men of Sombrunia do not drive their domestic beasts to feast upon the Dunenfels Plain. A taste of that grass makes them either sicken and die, or turn wild and break from their masters. The camels eat the grass without suffering any perceptible effects—but camels always were contrary creatures.

After sunset, Mustapha had Elcoloq perform around the fires of the camel drivers. It was generally agreed that the dog's antics were well worth his master's free passage. After the nightly entertainment, all the company pulled blankets around themselves and slept, to arise early the following day.

One night Mustapha had an odd and troubling dream. He felt as if he were asleep and awake at the same time. He saw himself sleeping on the ground, Elcoloq curled quietly by his side. A lady was there also, a most beautiful white lady with hair like cream and hands like milk. Pale as the moon was she, bearing only a red stain like a flower upon her bosom. She knelt beside the sleeping Mustapha and tried to wake him, but could not. His other self saw all this, powerless to do anything. The lady began to cry, sweet tears like April rain, and the sleeper slept on.

Then the lady looked up and turned her face toward the waking Mustapha. He felt himself hovering on the edge of recognition, but memory cheated him; fear overwhelmed knowledge. She sighed and vanished on the warm winds of the night.

Mustapha awoke in truth and looked frantically about him. The moon shone coldly down from her waning crescent and showed him nothing extraordinary in all the sleeping encampment. Elcoloq stirred heavily in his sleep and licked his master's hand; that was all. Deeply distressed, not knowing what the dream had meant, Mustapha lay staring at the heavens until sleep at last returned to him.

In the days that followed they crossed the Dunenfels Plain and the second range of mountains. These peaks were more difficult than the first, claiming five men and one camel in the snows atop the mountain passes. The second mountain range was one reason Sombrunia was so safe from attack by land, just as Vair's security rested in her mountains. The caravan picked out the beaten path down through the foothills and on a brilliant morning left the range behind them, starting across the arid stretches of the great Desert of Thulain.

Chapter X

DOG DAYS

In all the boiling vastness of the Desert of Thulain there is no relief to be found except beneath the palms of a few scattered oases. Barbarian Vahrd, the only known land besides Sombrunia and Vair in the southern climes, hugs itself tight to the second range of mountains through which caravans pass as they leave Sombrunia. It in turn is surrounded completely on the landward side by a slender arm of that same mountain chain. Tough, eager for booty, courageous in battle as the men of Vahrd may be, they shun the desert if they can.

A single people inhabits the Desert of Thulain. The men of Vair fear them greatly, the men of Sombrunia respect them, and the men of Vahrd hate them. Lord Olian leads these ravaging multitudes of the desert: They have no home, no fixed place of abode, but claim the entire desert as their own. Caravans pass only on their sufferance. The necessary bribes are paid to agents of Lord Olian in Vair and Sombrunia before a caravan driver even dreams of leaving. The raiders will spare only the soldiers of Sombrunia, for it is part of the training of these troopers to go alone into the desert and return with the heads of two of Olian's men before they can be admitted to the Sombrunian ranks.

The mountains of Vahrd had long been lost in the reddening west when the white lady again visited Mustapha. The caravan had thus far passed unmolested through the desert, and made camp that night at the Oasis of the Hidden Springs. The night wind of the desert was refreshingly cool at first, but wise men knew it would soon become frigid and bone chilling. Seasoned travelers wrapped themselves up well in their robes and blankets.

The visitation of the sorrowing specter was as it had been the first time. Again Mustapha awoke with a nameless dread in his heart. He felt strangely as if cool, moist hands had stroked his face. "It is only imagination," he told himself, but he slept no more that night.

The third visitation of the white lady occurred when the caravan stopped at the Oasis of the Sheepwell, and it was by far the most frightening of the phantom's appearances. Mustapha had not had a very calming day to start with. Elcoloq had long since run through all his repertoire of tricks, and the evening entertainments around the campfire were being received with lessening favor. He could not even teach Elcoloq any new tricks. The dog had possessed the gift of human speech for so long that he could learn nothing unless it was explained to him; then he had to ask questions about it. A caravan affords no privacy at all, so spoken conferences between master and dog were not feasible. The camel drivers became a more and more chilly audience.

Mustapha fell asleep after much tossing, only to have the pale apparition intrude upon his slumbers. He saw her weeping as usual, but now she tried to rouse him by shaking his shoulder and pulling at his blankets. The sleeping Mustapha slumbered through all her efforts. Still weeping, she arose and floated over the midnight sands to where Nailuj slept. With an expression of hate and horror on her face, the white lady touched the red stain on her breast and with the blood marked Nailuj's forehead. She pointed sternly at the old man and looked beseechingly toward the sleeping Mustapha; but what she wanted, he could not tell. Then she was gone.

Mustapha awoke with a shriek that roused the entire camp. The camel drivers muttered angrily, but on seeing the first red streaks of the new day on the horizon they bestirred themselves. Some approached Nailuj and held an earnest conversation with him. While they spoke, the still-trembling Mustapha beheld to his horror the faint shape of the white lady hovering momentarily above the head of Nailuj like a breath of mist in the morning. The specter threw her head back in a voiceless scream, then disappeared.

Nailuj did not seem to notice. The conference went on for a few moments more until he dismissed the camel drivers curtly and approached Mustapha, who was putting his things in order before loading them on the white camel.

"My son," said the old man gently, "what do you see over there, in the distance?"

Mustapha strained his eyes to the horizon. "I think I see the mountains of Vair." He smiled. "We shall be there tomorrow, I am sure."

"No," said Nailuj, looking 'deep into Mustapha's eyes, "we shall not. Perhaps I shall, but not you. Most assuredly, you shall not."

"What do you mean?" demanded Mustapha.

Nailuj spoke in a voice as tender as a mother's cradlesong. "Be calm, my son, be calm. All shall be revealed. Tell me, now, what is it that you see over there, a little before the mountains?"

Mustapha turned his eyes to the east again. "Tents," he said grimly. "It must be a Vairish caravan bound for Sombrunia."

"No," said Nailuj, "no caravan. It is a camp, the camp of Lord Olian's people, and there you shall stay all the days of your life."

"But why? Do you bring me here—you, who promised me friendship!—to sell me as a slave? What profit will you get for selling me to that barbarous and bloody terror of the desert?"

"'Barbarous and bloody terror of the desert'!" mocked Nailuj. "You speak like a man too long associated with bad poets. Barbarous and bloody and beastly and bold they call Lord Olian. Have you never thought they lied? Or exaggerated, at best?" Without waiting for an answer, Nailuj removed his turban, revealing pitchy black hair that contrasted boldly with his gray beard. "I am Olian."

That was when Elcoloq bit him.

The camel drivers, summoned by Lord Olian's furious yowls, pulled Elcoloq away and tied him up. Mustapha was likewise bound when he tried to interfere. Lord Olian bathed his wounds at the oasis pool and rinsed the dye out of his beard. He exchanged his modest merchant's robes for the more brilliant and serviceable scarlet trousers of a desert rider, but disdained the scorching sun, refusing shirt or cape. Barechested, he mounted the gloriously spirited roan stallion that his vassals led to him, and from the height of that splendid beast he spoke down to the helpless Mustapha.

"The poets call me barbarian!" he said, vastly amused. "Do they also tell of how we take our slaves? Do they say that we cannot purchase slaves in the free markets, and so must supply ourselves? The poets know nothing, and the few bards who have seen our ways will never sing of them except in our camps, for they are our slaves as well. You shall be as well cared for as any slave elsewhere, and we will give you ample time to teach your dog new tricks to amuse our children. If you do not, you shall become a work-slave and your dog will be trained to the hunt."

Having made this pronouncement, Lord Olian wheeled his horse sharply round and galloped off toward the distant tents. A grossly fat and surly camel driver who smelled like a dead goat now took charge of Mustapha and his wise dog. Elcoloq he tied by a stout rope to the heel of a camel; Mustapha he merely slung over the saddle, like a bale of hides.

Never in his life would Mustapha forget that last portion of his journey across the Desert of Thulain. A camel ride in a palanquin is one thing, but to have to bear a multitude of jerks and bumps with the bulge of a camel saddle pressing into your stomach and the sands of the universe thrown into your eyes with every step—that is not a ride to forget.

After an eternity had passed, Mustapha felt the camel stop, but he could not tell where he was, having a limited view of things from across the saddle. He was trundled down and set on his feet with little fuss, though his knees were so shaken that he could not stand steadily for a full three minutes. Elcoloq could not help him, being himself tied and exhausted after the long run.

They were in the middle of Lord Olian's camp. Brightly colored tents surrounded them. Men in loose white shirts and scarlet trousers emerged from the tents to pay homage to Olian. The desert lord sat upon a wooden throne of Vairish origin, part of the plunder of an especially rich caravan. The men knelt before him, and he lazily placed one foot on each man's lowered head in a ceremony of fealty. When the last of his men had thus done him service, Olian yawned and stood upon his throne.

"Now!" he bellowed, laughing. "Now let them come to me!"

There was an unearthly shriek and a scuffle of feet, then a small thunder as a mob of children stampeded from a score of tents and swarmed all over Lord Olian. The man was soon covered by his tiny assailants and brought to the ground with a crash while the little ones smothered him with every mark of affection they could bestow. Fights broke out within the infant throng between those who had gained Lord Olian's arms and those who could not yet reach his body. At last, shaking the kissing, clutching, crying, giggling babes off like so many raindrops, Lord Olian stood up in their midst. He reached down, picked up two little girls like twin roses, and came near Mustapha.

"They are all my children," he said. "These two in particular are my favorites, and it shall be them you must amuse with your wise dog. They are children of two mothers, but they might be twins. Look Shara! See, Sheena! What a pretty present Daddy has brought you today! Do you like it?" The little girls laughed and hid their faces in their father's shoulders, peeping at Mustapha shyly, then hiding again.

Mustapha was by no means surprised at Lord Olian's horde of children, having come from rather a large family himself. He did, of course, wonder that such a redoubtable warrior as Lord Olian chose two daughters for his favorites and not a son. Shara and Sheena wriggled free of their father and began to climb on Mustapha instead. Their slender childish fingers untied him with an ease usually found only in far older hands. Both had long, straight hair the color of foxes and the creamy skin of the northern lands. Only their eyes showed their father's influence. Their mothers had probably been slaves taken by the men of Braegerd Isle and sold to agents of Lord Olian. The barbarians of Braegerd had no qualms about dealing with the desert hordes. In their swift longships they rode the waves of the sea as ruthlessly as Lord Olian's men rode the dunes of the desert.

Mustapha was a diplomatic man; that is to say, he knew which way the wind blew and ducked accordingly. He therefore bowed before the two little princesses of the desert and begged their leave to show them great wonders. The girls giggled and would not answer until a look from Olian—at once stern and loving—told them this was not the way ladies of their station should behave. Shara, the bolder of the two, bade Mustapha bring forth his miracles. Mustapha fetched Elcoloq for the delighted children.

There was no question that Mustapha's position as player-slave was secure after Elcoloq's performance. Sheena embraced the dog around the neck and Shara held Mustapha's hand with real affection when the act was over.

"You approve, my daughters?" asked Lord Olian.

"We approve," said Shara with piping dignity.

"Good, for if you ever find this man an unsatisfactory entertainer, he shall become a work-slave. His dog likewise will learn new ways to earn his keep."

"No," said Sheena, joining her half-sister in princely hauteur. "We will not have that. The man and the dog are ours. We shall teach them new tricks if we must. Let no one interfere with them, on pain of our displeasure. Come." This last was addressed to Mustapha, who allowed himself and his dog to be led off by his petite patronesses. Lord Olian smiled, pleased.

Chapter XI

DOG-TROT

The fate of a slave is the fate of his master. Mustapha knew this well. Even when he was a youth and had considered becoming the slave of his brothers, he had known it. The state in which a slave lives is almost as fine as that of his master. The rich who keep slaves want them to shine forth as living examples of their masters' wealth; even so, Mustapha couldn't help marveling at Lord Olian's fantastic wealth.

Shara and Sheena, favorites of the desert lord, each had her own tent, both made of cool green silk and supported by ornate poles inset with gold and emeralds. Shara informed her nurse that Sheena would move into her tent so that their new playfellow might live in Sheena's tent. The word of the princess was obeyed. But the nurse, who knew where to draw the line, overruled the girls' attempt to take Elcoloq into their tent.

"Slave," called Shara.

Mustapha knelt before her.

"Let me hear your commands, O princess," he said. At most she was eight years old, but as his owner she could have him beheaded if he disobeyed or displeased her.

"Slave, you sleep there," she said, pointing to the tent. "Two guards will watch you. Your dog will stay with you. You shall eat with us tonight; so shall your dog." With no further ceremony, the girls scampered into the other green tent. Mustapha heard them giggling within and Shara asking Sheena whether she had spoken fiercely enough to the slave.

Two enormous guards bearing two equally enormous

swords escorted Mustapha and Elcoloq into their tent. The furnishings were luxurious, extremely so. Everything that could be made of metal was gold or silver; everything that could be made of cloth was silk and satin and airiest gauze. Elcoloq found the best pillow in the tent and laid claim to it while Mustapha reclined upon the divan.

"This, then, is what the white lady tried to warn me of," said Mustapha dejectedly, helping himself to a pomegranate from a brimming fruit bowl. "Slavery! To think I should come to this!"

"What's wrong, master?" asked Elcoloq, grinning. "Now we need go no further in our quest. Why should I ever have to steal again, seeing how well we shall be provided for? We need not find my cure in unknown lands. I am quite content." He stretched out and yawned, rolling onto his back with lazy abandon.

"Of course you would not understand, being but a dumb beast," said Mustapha. "You know not the meaning of the word *slavery*."

"On the contrary," said the dog. "I, better than any, ought to know what it means. Many ages have come and gone since your race introduced mine to the meaning of that word in its most binding sense. Aye, and so many centuries have passed since that day that now my people do not know any other existence. We even mourn when we are deprived of our state of servitude. So you will get used to it. We did."

"You? You are a dog, speaking of dogs! I am a man, and men suffer and feel more the yoke of slavery than other animals. We understand it!"

"If you understand it so well," said Elcoloq, "then you must understand how terrible it is to be enslaved. Yet you do not stop enslaving us. No, nor stop enslaving your own kind, men like ourselves!"

"Be still," said Mustapha, muttering against all dogs who meddled in things they knew nothing of. Elcoloq overheard him.

"Do not think me entirely ignorant, master," he said. "You think that dogs and cats and other beasts are truly dumb, but I assure you, there is more said in a single dog's lonely baying at the moon than in all the volumes of poetry that the great scribe Azhdi ever wrote."

"Mindless music," countered Mustapha, "such as children make on kitchen pans. That is all the dogs say in their howling."

"You think so," said Elcoloq, "because of what the gods have ordained. I will tell you how the mastery of man over the other beasts came about and what it is the dogs all sing when they howl at the moon.

"In the beginning of the beasts, master, no animal was higher than his brother, not even man. Each creature found the thing he loved to do the best and worked at it, living in peace and contentment. The cats danced the slow dances of sinuous grace; the birds learned the serenades of dawn; and men delighted to squat in the mud by the riverbank, making little figures out of clay and parading them about while they told terrible lies, thinking the figures alive.

"Only the wise beasts felt the divine hunger for something greater than the pleasant life that flowed from day to day into the sea of death. Oh, yes, we died in those days as in these, but always in dreams the animals would pass away, wakening to the true world of spirit. As I said, only the wise beasts wanted something more. There is no sin in such hunger.

"They were four, the wise beasts of the earth: the lion, whose might and majesty were even then admired; the horse, whose solid good sense earned him the name Heeni—Wise Counselor; the cow, whose heart was free of selfish desires; and the dog, who brimmed over with a happy energy that made him dash here and there, place to place, always seeking.

"The gods still walked the earth in those times. It was the happy era, before the double birth that brought bitter death and violence into the world, before the struggle that still rages and will someday end forever. The lion called his three comrades to him and addressed them in this way:

"'Brothers, we are the only ones who feel a void within us, an emptiness that food can never fill nor water make quiet. I have measured the earth with the strides of my paws and have not found the thing I seek. I do not even know what it is.'

"'You will know it when you find it,' replied Heeni. 'That much is certain. We shall all know it when we find it.'

"'We shall know it with a sureness of the heart,' added

the cow, turning her large and beautiful eyes toward the lion.

"'I will find it for us all. I! I! I!' yapped the dog. He could not be still for a moment, not even at such an important meeting. He sprang to his paws, sat, sprang up again, trotted nervously around the three other beasts, made little sprints into the forest that surrounded them, and came back again.

"'Peace, brethren,' said the lion, raising up one golden-tufted paw. 'I have our answer at hand. We shall find the gods themselves and ask it of them.'

"This pronouncement threw the others into a turmoil of words and objections. They knew the gods and loved them, but the power of those blessed beings was too overwhelming for the simple animals to face. They could never bring themselves to address the gods. They only spoke to them when the gods spoke first.

"The wise Heeni shook his long head slowly from side to side and churned up the earth with his hooves. 'No,' he said. 'We cannot do this. The gods are too great. They may be angry. They may destroy us.'

"'Do not fear,' said the lion with a smile. 'I have a plan. None of us shall ask the question of the gods. Let us pick another animal, a stupid one, and have him do it. If the gods are angry, he shall be punished, not us.'

"The others conferred and agreed that it was a good idea. They did not spare a thought of pity for the stupid animal they would send as their messenger, not even the kindly cow. This was the first great sin of the world. They debated and argued for a long time over which animal was the stupidest, and at last narrowed down the contenders to two. The lion said it was the sheep; the dog said man.

"'Sheep are so placid, so dull!' said the lion. 'They wander the fields as if they had forgotten something and cannot remember what it is or what it looks like or even if they really need it. They never question anything, roaming the meadows in their herds, each sheep just as silly as his leader.'

"'You have hit it!' cried the dog. 'They are silly, but not stupid. They ask no questions, as you say. Will the gods not be suspicious to have the sheep come to them with a question now? No, let us send a man. Men are just as silly as sheep; they follow their leaders just as blindly. They do no work that profits any of us, but waste their days playing with the little clay figures they mold by the riverbank. We must feed them or they starve. If the gods punish men, it will be no great loss to us.' This cruelty was the second great sin of the world.

"So the four wise beasts agreed to send a man to the gods with their question and their hunger. The dog went down to the riverbank and called to one of the men who sat naked in the mud, playing with the clay figurines.

"'Child of earth and water!' he called. 'Come here, I have work for you!' The man reluctantly left his earthen dolls to attend the dog. 'The lion, the horse, the cow, and I all bid you go to the gods and ask them this question,' said the dog. 'Do not forget a word of it or you will suffer. Ask the gods this: "We hunger for what we cannot see. We search for what we do not know. What is the thing we long for? Give it to us now, or tell us where it lies."' The dog went over the question several times until the man got it right.

"The man, whose name was Virhom, left the riverbank where his fellows still played with the clay figures and went into the forest. He wandered through the trees, ever repeating the question so that he would not forget it. Every night before he slept he repeated it, and every morning when he awoke. He traveled for days and days, but never met the gods.

"At last he encountered one of the gods in the forest, and to his eternal good fortune it was the merciful, the beautiful, the divine Ambra, goddess of the light-in-darkness, kindest of the gods. Of all the gods, Ambra loved men the most out of the multitudes of creatures on the earth. Many say this was because her divine mother gave the infant Ambra to be cared for by the first man. In gratitude, the good goddess created for him the first woman. These may be only stories.

"Ambra smiled, and the man fell down before her. 'Mighty One,' he said, 'I have come to ask you a question.' He made no other attempt at courtesy, for men were always plain-spoken.

"'Ask it,' said Ambra. So the man stood up and boldly asked the goddess the question that the four beasts had given him, but he never said that the question was theirs and not his.

"Ambra listened, then spread her silver wings and stretched her white arms toward heaven. 'Child of my heart,' she said, 'there are many things unseen that you might be searching for. Which is it that you want? Is it love or wisdom? Is it truth or contentment? Is it power to rule the world or power to rule yourself? Tell me, and it is yours.'

"The man was overjoyed at this sweet reply of the goddess. Alas, he had no idea how to choose the thing that the animals wanted. He remained silent at her generosity.

"'Well,' said Ambra, when the man would not speak, 'if you have no preference, I shall give you the gift that is the easiest to use, although it is not the best to have. You are a simple creature, content to play with your figures of clay beside the river. You make them go here and there at your bidding. I shall give you the gift of power over others, child of my heart. Use it well and it will lead you to the other gifts of the gods. Use it foolishly and it will return you to the mud of the riverbank.'"

"Then Ambra drew a frail glass vial from the folds of her starlit robes and told Virhom to drink from it. Strange fires raced through his veins, and suddenly the riverbank seemed to him to be a ridiculous place to play with little clay figures. He would use living things for his games! He would send them here and there at his will! He would leave the mud of the riverbank and command all the sprawling lands of the earth. Ambra saw the change in his face and her heart was pained, realizing what a grave mistake she had made in giving man the gift of power. But then she consoled herself, remembering that Virhom was still young and hoping that age would bring him the wisdom necessary to use his powers better. She returned to the stars.

"The four animals were waiting at the edge of the forest for Virhom to return. But Virhom had grown cunning. He made the first magic in the world, for magic is power. Four stones he took and four vines from a tree, saying words of binding over them. He would begin his domination of the world by capturing the four wise beasts.

"Like a snake, Virhom slithered on his belly through the low brush around the clearing where the four animals waited.

He threw his first stone and it struck the kindly cow, leaving her frozen until he could slip the vine rope around her neck and lead her away. The second stone struck Heeni, the horse, and affected him the same way. He was a horse of stone.

"The dog and the lion bounded to their feet when they saw what had happened to their comrades. Fear seized them, and the lion roared with rage at what he could not see to fight. 'Coward, come out!' he bellowed. 'Come out and face me! I will tear your flesh from your bones and drink your blood if you try to conquer me!'

"The man heard the lion's roar and trembled. He wanted power, but he wanted it with safety. He shook so much that he dropped the magic stone and the magic leash with which he had meant to capture the lion. Both fell into a patch of wheat growing wild on the edge of the clearing. Virhom arose from the bushes and confronted the lion and the dog, thinking to capture them with cunning instead.

"'My brothers,' said the man, 'I have returned from the gods with your question answered. Come closer, that I may tell it to you.' He wished to capture the lion with his last stone and let the dog go free. Virhom saw more use for the lion than for the dog. But the lion was too wise for him. He would not move.

"Alas, the dog was foolish. He thought the man was still the stupidest of beasts. He did not suspect this dull creature of having enchanted his two friends, and so he trotted closer to hear the answer to his question. The lion, still bristling with anger and suspicion, bounded away into the forest.

"The man saw the lion escape, and so he struck the hapless dog with the magic stone and bound him with the magic rope. 'Because I have lost my prey, I shall work you twice as hard,' said the man. 'You shall help me hunt and tame all the other beasts of the world. You shall be with me always, in my fields and in my houses. Now come, for we have a world to conquer.'

"So the man made the dog his most heavily worked slave, and with his help he enslaved the other beasts. He may ride the horse into battles, and he may depend on the cow and the wheat plant for his food; but it is always the dog who remains at his side, even to the gates of death. Man has forgotten much, but we dogs never shall. Each night we turn our muzzles to the moon and howl for the woe of slavery, telling to the stars the tale of Virhom's treachery and our own foolish pride."

Outside the rippling green walls of silk the light grew fainter. Evening was coming, and the delicate emerald tent surrounding the wanderers became as dark as the soul of the sea. A woman, likewise a slave, brought them their dinner. She was a pretty maiden, though very filthy from all her work around the cookfires. Mustapha sighed after her when she was gone.

"Cheer up, master!" teased Elcoloq. "It may be that your owners will allow you to have her for your wife when they need more little slaves, so long as they get the pick of the litter!"

"Atrocious beast, be still!" thundered Mustapha.

"As you wish, but the leash is on the other neck now, isn't it?" mocked the dog. After that they ate dinner in silence.

After dinner they were called upon to entertain. Elcoloq held back his most spectacular tricks, as Mustapha had suggested. The longer Lord Olian's people thought the dog was learning new tricks—really old ones revealed—the longer it would be before Elcoloq actually had to learn new ones. They received no applause, but since they were slaves this lack of approving show was customary. Certain of Lord Olian's high officers later sent Mustapha gold and a few gems as silent praise of the act, while children delivered gifts of food for the dog. A popular entertainer-slave might earn enough in gifts to eventually buy his freedom.

"A good show," said Mustapha, counting the take while Elcoloq demolished a haunch of wild desert pig. "We could be out of here in less than two years, if we try." He hid the treasure and went to sleep.

That night the white lady returned. She passed through the silken tent like wind and knelt beside Mustapha. This time he saw her, but did not see his own sleeping form. Then he knew that he was not dreaming any longer, but saw the specter in reality. The mark of blood on her bosom looked a thousand times more scarlet than before, and the tears upon her cheeks were all of silver.

"Who are you?" wondered Mustapha in a whisper. "Why do you visit me? Was it to warn me? To help me? Who are you?"

The ghost's translucent face swam before his eyes as the tears vanished and a look of anger took their place. Mustapha cowered, fearing the vengeful spirit and feeling also the greater fear of not knowing why the phantom should be enraged with him. The wavering white figure raised its fists high in the air, clenched in a gesture of wrath, while Mustapha trembled, waiting for the otherworldly punishment to fall.

"Oooh!" moaned the apparition, but Mustapha saw that its anger was not directed toward him after all. A second phantom had appeared beside the white lady, and it was to this one that the wandering spirit turned in fury. "I told you that you should have let me speak to him, you fool! I never was any good at pantomime, and you know it! And after all this dear man did for us, you wouldn't even let me tell him about Lord Olian's disguise when he might have escaped safely back to Sombrunia. No, I had to float around and point in a dramatic fashion and hope he'd understand. Brilliant! That's what comes of listening to you, Polkin!"

The white lady spoke with exasperation to the smaller ghost that had joined her beside Mustapha's divan. Elcoloq was awake now, too, and eagerly sniffed at the pair of spirits, wagging his tail. Man's memory is short, his other senses dim, but a dog can follow the scent of a friend or enemy even beyond the bounds of life itself. Now Elcoloq fawned and pranced before the white lady, whom he had recognized as his dear and long-lost friend Gatica.

"But, dearest," protested the late, great Polkin, "it just isn't done! Where have you ever seen a ghost warn someone of danger in words? Nowhere! The phantom *always* communicates in dumbshow."

"Dumb," said Gatica, "sums it up. If you had only let me say in so many words, 'Mustapha, this old codger who calls himself Nailuj is really Olian of the Desert Hordes, so flee for your life and freedom!' our friend would not be a slave now. It is my punishment for listening to you. In fact, listening to you was what brought about our deaths in the first place, and that's *your* punishment!"

Mustapha was loath to interrupt a domestic quarrel, but his surprise at seeing his former companions made him forget all manners. He tried to embrace them and grasped empty air. Gatica gave him a kiss that passed through one cheek and touched the other. Indeed it is very hard to show any physical sign of affection for ghosts, no matter how dear they may have been in life. Mustapha's attempts to hug them did produce the happy effect of stopping their quarrel and getting their attention back to more important matters.

"Mustapha, my friend," said Polkin, "this life of a slave is not for you. Your life is the freedom of the road, the merrymaking of country fair and tavern. You must escape."

"Gladly," Mustapha agreed. "But how?" He waited for Polkin to give him some supernatural wisdom that would miraculously deliver him.

"By running away," answered Polkin.

Mustapha was crushed. "That's all?"

"There is no more to it." Polkin shrugged. "How could there be? It is a simple matter. You watch for your chance and you run away. Head southwest, if you like. There is an oasis there somewhere."

"But—but aren't you going to transport me? Or levitate me? Or conjure me elsewhere?"

"What? Come, Mustapha, that only happens in stories! If we cannot do so much as shake hands with you, how will we do anything else? All we can do is advise you a bit."

"Ha!" sneered Elcoloq.

"It is better than nothing, dog," said Polkin. "And it is all we can do. You may take it or leave it. But if you leave it, remember that the day will come when they will tire of your tricks and put you to real work, so be warned."

"I suppose it is better than nothing," Mustapha sighed. "Will you do us one favor? Go out and tell me where the guards are."

"I looked," said Gatica. "They flank the door."

"Could you bring me a knife to slit the back of the tent?"

"How? I could not even lift— Oh, wait! I do believe we can help you after all. Gatica!" Polkin tried to snap his misty fingers. "We shall give these guards a little show. Prepare to bid farewell to Olian forever and be ready to run, Mustapha. Gatica, we perform *The Murder of Rosella!*" Gatica smiled consent and the phantoms vanished.

Everyone knows that the death scene from *The Murder of Rosella* is the most horrific moment in all drama. Children are not permitted to attend performances of this work, nor are maidens and youths allowed to see it unless they are betrothed. In the southern lands no woman of any sort, unless she is over seventy years of age, may see it. Sometimes those who do watch the play wish that they had not, only because of this death scene. Even when it is poorly acted, it has its effect. No wonder, then, that within a few moments Mustapha heard the brawny guards begin to scream like terrified infants, then heard the sound of their scurrying flight across the sands. With Elcoloq behind him, Mustapha shot out of the now unguarded tent and into the moonlit reaches of the Desert of Thulain.

Chapter XII

HOT DOG

Mustapha and his wise dog fled the camp of Lord Olian in hurry but not in haste. A man of the southern lands by birth, Mustapha had much respect for the great Desert of Thulain. Had someone assured him a thousand times that an oasis was five minutes' walk from where he stood, had he even seen the palms and caught a glimpse of cool water beneath their shade, still he would have taken the time to seize provisions and fill a waterskin before taking a step across the dunes. Nothing man could inflict upon him—not slavery itself—could have made Mustapha neglect those precautions. The desert is more treacherous than man.

Likewise, there was nothing man could inflict upon him that would be more ironically cruel and cunning than the half-buried rock over which he tripped that night. It was a very small stumble, but it was a fatal one, for as he picked himself up he caught the waterskin on the edge of the rock and put a microscopic tear in it. It was a trifling tear, a tear of such small size that he did not notice it when he put the waterskin to his lips to drink. But in the Desert of Thulain there is no such thing as an insignificant tear in your waterskin.

"Strange," said Mustapha as he let Elcoloq lap water from his cupped hands. "I would swear the skin is lighter than it ought to be. We have not drunk that much from it."

"It must be your imagination," said the dog when he finished lapping up the water. "Let us go on. We shall be at the first oasis by the time the waterskin is empty."

There was truth in Elcoloq's words. Already they saw a distant speck on the desert that ought to have been their goal. The waterskin, however, ran out a day's march from the oasis.

"Bah, it is nothing!" said a thirsty Mustapha as they drank from the pool. "I miscalculated. Our next stop shall be the Oasis of the Quails, and this time I shall make certain to fill the waterskin to the top."

A day and a half before they reached the second oasis, they ran out of water. This time Mustapha blamed it on the shepherd they had questioned at the first oasis. The old man had probably underestimated the distance between oases.

"Age makes all walks shorter," said Mustapha. "At the Oasis of the Quails I will ask more than one person about distances before we proceed. Curse Lord Olian! If it were not for him, we might have entered Vair by the nearer mountain pass. As it stands, we must skirt around the mountains like thieves and take a farther gap into the sweet land." He sighed with longing for Vair as he filled the waterskin. This time they spent a full two days of thirst upon the sands.

At the Oasis of the Bent Willow, which lies outside the southwestern border of Vair, they fell in with some merchants and spent a few days in their company while the caravan rested. Mustapha was more cautious with his words after his escape from Lord Olian, not trusting the merchants overmuch even though they spoke the Vairish tongue and claimed to come from near his old village of Basha. The three merchantmen—Mani, Mota, and Jaqar—were brothers, sons of the famous merchant-prince Pepi. They extended fine hospitality to Mustapha and Elcoloq.

"Travel with us," said Mani. "We go to Sombrunia, but then we return to Vair. It will be a longer journey than you hope for, but surely a safer one. Even when you stand within sight of the beloved and blessed mountains, you are not entirely safe."

"Nay, I thank you," said Mustapha. "We have not much time; we will go on alone."

"The pass by which we came from Vair through the august and benevolent mountains lies not far from here," said Mota. "With a full waterskin you should reach it in two days at most."

"What are you saying, fool!" said Jaqar. "The two days' trip is toward the next oasis, and that oasis lies a week's trek from the pass. Because the land grows kindlier from the oasis to the pass, it seems like no time at all."

This dispute went on between the brothers until Mustapha was totally confused as to precisely how far they were from the coveted mountain pass. Fortunately, the three brothers did agree as to the direction of the next oasis.

"All that is needful are provisions and water," said Jaqar.

"Well, then we have nothing to fear," said Mustapha, smiling down at the generous sack of provender that the merchants had given him to accompany his trusty waterskin. He patted the waterskin proudly, as he would a comrade who had shared the journey across the desert. He did not look at it or see the ever-so-tiny tear that was growing ever-so-slightly larger, while an almost invisible trickle of water ran down the side of the skin and was sucked up greedily by the golden sands. Such a tiny tear! Such an unimportant little flaw!

Mustapha and Elcoloq slept the final day before the caravan went on, preferring to brave the chill of the desert night rather than the heat of the desert day. Three hours before dawn, Mustapha filled the waterskin brimful and bade farewell to the Oasis of the Bent Willow.

A caravan makes better time than a single man on foot, despite all the coordination it takes to get it started. Two days' travel for a caravan is considerably more for a man alone, especially if the waterskin he carries suddenly and inexplicably splits open on the fourth day. Mustapha and Elcoloq gazed dumbly as their last few drops of water spurted out of the bag and into the insatiable gullet of the Desert of Thulain.

"How did it happen?" asked the dog.

"I know not," said Mustapha. "And if I knew, it would make no difference now. But let us be glad, for I think I see the oasis over there."

"Aye," Elcoloq agreed. "And I can even see the mountains."

So Mustapha and his wise dog set out for the oasis that beckoned them so sweetly just beyond the next dune. They reached it not that day, nor yet the next. A host of days they trod over the harsh sands and still the oasis beckoned from afar, laughing in the shelter of its palms. Mustapha was at length compelled to carry Elcoloq; the poor beast could go no farther on his own.

"Master," begged the dog, his tongue lolling, "I implore you, slay me that you may have some nourishment. It is to cure me that you are forced to this place. It is my fault. Let me here atone for it."

"Foolish dog," chided Mustapha. "It is to cure you we came, so why should you die? A strange cure! Speak of it no more. I still have an orange left in my sack. Lap up the juice and you will feel better."

"Better," panted Elcoloq, ignoring the tempting fruit. "For how long? Look, Mustapha!" And the dog heavily swayed his snout to the east, where a cloud had obscured the oasis from sight. "A sandstorm," said Elcoloq. "We are lost."

"Maybe," said Mustapha, forcing the dog to drink from the orange. He then picked him up again and strode forward, toward the approaching storm. "But if our doom comes, let us meet it."

It was not a long sandstorm, but it was a bitter one. Mustapha drew his hood tightly over his nose and mouth and wrapped Elcoloq under the loose folds of his robes. The dog, weak as a bundle of rags, let his master do what he liked with him. They moved on, into the heart of the storm. When the stinging wind grew too strong to battle, Mustapha crouched down and hoped the storm would pass before it could bury them.

There is infinity in the shifting of the sands. Eternity is held in a single hourglass as long as there is a hand to turn it, to let the sands flow constantly, gently, forever back and forth, whispering away the hours. Think, then, of the thousands of small forevers that Mustapha passed while the sands of a greater hourglass turned by a greater hand flowed and whispered around him—flowed, whispered, and finally stopped.

Slowly Mustapha lifted up his head, shaking off the sand. With difficulty he straightened up, not so much because of the small hillock of sand the storm had heaped upon him as because of the stiffness in his limbs from having remained hunched over for so long. Once free of his golden prison, he removed the folds of cloth that protected his eyes and looked around, then gave a gasp of delight. Swiftly he took

Elcoloq out from beneath his robes, almost too excited for words.

"Behold, my friend!" he cried gladly. "See what the beneficent gods have done for us! Drink, now. Drink, best of animals. There is plenty to be had."

Elcoloq staggered forward and fell down, muzzle first, into the most beautiful, the most pellucid, the most cooling pool of honeyed water in all the Desert of Thulain. After the first ravenous gulping, the wise dog moderated his thirst, knowing full well that too much zeal in drinking after too long an abstinence will kill beast or man surer than thirst itself. When he had had his fill, he looked around.

Mustapha still lay on his belly, drinking eagerly from the pool. Over his head Elcoloq saw such heavily laden palms, swayed by the weight of the dates they bore, that it was a miracle they did not topple down. Beyond the palms was a little orchard of orange, pomegranate, and other fruit trees. Snowy sheep grazed peacefully in the shade of the branches.

"Good master, where have we come?" asked Elcoloq when Mustapha finished drinking.

"Why, to the oasis our friends told us of, naturally," said Mustapha, filling his sack with dates and oranges. "Where do you think we should be?"

"But, master, look!" urged Elcoloq, pulling at Mustapha's robes until the man faced north. "They said we could see the mountains of Vair from this oasis. Where are the mountains?"

Mustapha looked. There were no mountains to the north, nor to the south, either—nor to the east or west. All about the heavenly oasis stretched the sullen sands. There was not even the sign of a shepherd's hut in all that blazing, angry vastness. The sheep bleated contentedly in the orchard, but no one tended them. The trees bore wondrous fruits, but no keeper of the orchard could be seen. Where were the mountains? Where was the land of Vair? Where had they come to in their lonesome wanderings?

"Master," said Elcoloq gently, "we were very thirsty, were we not?" Mustapha nodded. "And it was a very bad storm, wasn't it?" Again Mustapha agreed. "It lasted long, very long," said the dog. "It might still be lasting. And we, good master, might have been buried by it. O master, master! This is a place of plenty and peace! Master, are we dead?"

Chapter XIII

DOGSBODY

"Dead? Did you hear that, Bliss? The silly things think they are dead! Isn't that funny?"

"Oh, yes, Wildrose. But I have always found them funny. I have always said so. Haven't I?"

Mustapha and Elcoloq looked around them in sudden fear at these strange, mocking voices. The oasis was unchanged. Still the pool sparkled, the sheep grazed, the trees bent beneath their loads of fruit.

"Ho! Now they are looking for us! Shall I help them, Beloved? Or shall I let them wait and wonder?"

"Oh, do show yourself, Bliss! You are the most beautiful of us all. Surely *she* will not mind it this once. We must bring them before her anyway, and we'll all have to show ourselves eventually. Isn't that right, Starlight?"

"I agree; let it be Bliss. Bliss is so much more impressive, but that's only because she is you-know-who's best toady. Isn't that right, Wildrose?"

"Well, then, I will reveal myself, if you insist. You *do* insist?"

By now Mustapha and his wise dog were whirling about like crazy planets, seeking everywhere for the source of the golden voices that seemed to come from all sides. Dizzy, they sat down and awaited what the voices should decide to do.

"At least we aren't dead," said Elcoloq helpfully.

"Not yet," said Mustapha. "But—"

Then the great wings blossomed out before his eyes into glittering sheets of jeweled flame and a face more lovely, more exquisite than music gazed down upon him from a giddy height. The being of the shining wings hovered graceful and serene in the limpid desert air, its small white feet more beautiful than the love of mortal women, its long black hair held back in diamond fillets, its slender form clothed in ruby-colored light. Mustapha fell upon his face before it. Elcoloq groveled in fear and worship.

"Oh, do get up, you funny creatures! Can't you, please?" said the vision.

"Of course they can't, Bliss. You really are a goose at times. Don't you see you've scared them?" Another gloriously shining being joined Bliss in the air, having shaken off her disguise as one of the oasis sheep.

"Beloved is right! Aren't you, Beloved?" interjected a third presence, whose apparition coincided with the disappearance of a pomegranate tree.

"What shall we do, Starlight?"

"Why not ask Wildrose?"

"But isn't Laughter older?"

"What difference does age make, Ecstasy?"

The air became filled with a sweet chatter of music and the whir of many pairs of fiery wings. The constant questioning and bickering went on for some time before Mustapha and Elcoloq dared to look up. They beheld an awesome spectacle indeed. At least a score of creatures, each as fair and majestic as the first, had joined their royal sister in the air, and all were talking at once. Though the words were foolish, the dulcet harmonies of their voices made their constant prattle sound like the wisdom of the world.

"Oh, look, Pearl, they've gained courage. Aren't they sweet?" exclaimed a winged being whose robe was made entirely of flowers. She turned out to be Wildrose, of course.

In fact, all the fair ones were wrapped in splendors that echoed their names. Pearl was covered with the precious sea gems; Starlight was sheathed in cold, white glory; Beloved was robed in untellable tenderness that somehow took material form; Ecstasy was almost too brilliant to behold.

"Who are you, and what manner of place is this?" asked Mustapha. A full one-third of the trees from the orchard were gone, returned to their original form as these magnificent creatures. All of the sheep had resumed their proper, so-much-more-splendid shape as well.

"Who are we? Where are we?" echoed Laughter, her very dress twinkling with merriment. "Why do you ask?"

"Have you not heard of us? Who are you, for that matter?" asked Peace, dressed in the blue of a calm sky.

"Master!" exclaimed Elcoloq, "I know who they are! I have heard the bards sing of them in the courtyards of castles, and I have heard bad poets recite doggerel about them in the worst of taverns. They are peris! It cannot be otherwise. And yet I thought the race of peris dead."

"Peris? Who speaks our name? Who knows us?" earnestly asked Wisdom.

"It was the dog, my sister," replied Laughter. "What are we to do now? What are Her Majesty's orders? Did she say anything about talking dogs?"

"She said to bring any men who came here before her, after we had learned their business. She would then deal with them accordingly," said Wisdom sagely. "But what of dogs?"

"Did she mention dogs?" asked Pearl.

"She did not *not* mention them. And if this one talks, does it make him a man?" wondered Beloved.

"I think they both count as men, though maybe we should take them both to Her Majesty and let her decide?"

"Her Majesty!" Mustapha interrupted. "What queen is powerful enough to command such charming legions? She can be no other than Queen Nahrit. Elcoloq, we have found the place we sought when we least expected to find it! O most beautiful peris, fairest of the daughters of earth and angels! Take us, we beseech you, before your queen."

The peris were momentarily silent at Mustapha's request. However, nothing will keep a peri silent for long. Soon enough they resumed their strange and witless debate about Mustapha and Elcoloq.

"He asks to go before her. She has ordered that he be brought before her. Is obeying one obeying the other? Are we to obey mortals?" asked Excellence.

The peris' decision made perfect sense—to a peri. They resolved to take Mustapha and Elcoloq to the queen so that she could take a look at them and decide whether or not she would see them. Allowing her ivory feet to touch the sands, Starlight scooped up Mustapha and his wise dog in the palm of one hand. Upon touching the earth she grew larger than she had been in the air. Her fingers curved around the mortal creatures like the most perfect alabaster pillars of a king's pleasure palace. Like a flock of phoenixes, the peris flew away to the south, bearing Mustapha and Elcoloq deep into the heart of the desert.

With a flutter of flames they landed. This time when their glimmering feet touched the earth, the peris shrank to the height of mortal women. Mustapha imagined himself transported to some potentate's harem, so hemmed in by beauty on all sides was he. Yet when Beloved and Laughter placed their hands on his shoulders to urge him on, the pleasant spell was broken. Their creamy fingers bit cruelly into his flesh, and a terrible strength in their supple arms propelled him forward. Forward he went, still walking on the sands of the Desert of Thulain. Then his feet became aware of a subtle difference. Elcoloq, whining eagerly, noticed it as well.

"See, master, there is more than sand beneath our feet," said the dog. "Here and there I think I perceive some vestige of paving stones under the dusting of sand. And are those not bounding stones, such as some kingdoms use?"

It was true. Small knobs of regularly spaced red stones protruded from the sand to either side of them. In certain lands of the Twelve Kingdoms it was the custom to use such bounding stones to distinguish the royal highways from the common thoroughfares. Trotting along, Elcoloq stopped to investigate one of the stones and rushed back to Mustapha, yapping excitedly.

"Master, these are no ordinary stones. They are carved of garnet, each one! They were statues once. They have been worn down a bit, but still I can see the traces of the figures they once were: figures of men!"

"What a clever dog, isn't he?" said Hyacinth. "Good boy. Do come back now, or I'll pinch you. Do you know why those stones bear such a shape?"

"Loveliest One, I plead ignorance. Enlighten me," said Mustapha, relapsing completely into the excesses of the Vairish tongue. To the peris it did not matter whether Mustapha addressed them in the language of Vair, Sombrunia, Vahrd, or the Common of the northern lands. All languages

were one to them, and their language insinuated its way into
the brain of a man so that he understood it as if he had been
born speaking it.

"They are men," said Hyacinth. "Or, at any rate, once
they were. See how small some of them have become!
But look closely, mortal, and you shall see wonders. The
sands can never erase their form or features. Each year
they dwindle, but never does their agony blur. But who
should know more of timeless suffering than we? We share
their punishment as we shared their crime, and yet I think
that mortals have forgotten them as they have forgotten
us. Is this so?"

Mustapha passed one hand before his eyes in the traditional gesture of accepting blame. "May my eyes no longer
see the sun if I lie to you. It is true. Who were these men,
and what crime was so great to punish them in this manner?"

"And us, mortal!" Wisdom prompted. "Shall Harmony
sing to you the *Ballad of the Stones?*"

Mustapha bowed.

The peris were happy to break the monotony of the journey with song. Each of those fascinating beings plucked a
musical instrument of some kind from the air and struck up
a melody of unguessed sweetness while Harmony sang:

"Fair days and old are gone past all regretting,
Yet there can be no way of our forgetting.
O peris! O ye daughters of the air!
Sing, sing again of what a fall was there!

High sit the gods, high sit they at their pleasure.
Low, low sit men, who envy them their treasure.
Between the two, between the two we fly
Who cannot weep and who can never die.

In ancient days, when men were born to wonder,
There lived a king whose sword was forged in
    thunder,
Whose crown was made of stars, whose royal throne
Was of a mountain carved, of living stone.

With justice did he rule, with open hand.
O sisters, we were glad of his command!

And yet we listened, foolish peris we,
Unto the words we heard beside the sea.

He stood beside the waves, upon the shore,
The king's own minister and chancellor,
And spoke in honeyed words, in accents sweet,
In words that drew the peris to his feet.

The king, he said, had ruled us all too long.
His face, his voice, his arm no more were strong.
Why should the peris, why should men be swayed?
Why should a feeble ruler be obeyed?

He spoke, we heeded; him we followed fast,
Both men and peris, thinking that at last
We should be kings! The king should serve us all!
O there, my sisters, there began our fall!

Fallen the chancellor who told us lies,
Fallen the peris, never more to rise,
But doomed to serve whoever may us find
And hold our magics in the spells that bind.

Fallen the men as well, but soft their fate.
So wise a king can never rule with hate.
Some asked his pardon; this he freely gave.
Yet some, before their king, did think it brave

To stand with hearts defiant, sword in hand,
As if that king a sword could not withstand!
Thus spake the king: 'As ye will not atone,
But stand hardhearted, ye shall be as stone.

'Stones shall ye be to line the royal way,
And thus to stand forever till the day
That love shall touch ye, touch your hardened hearts.
Then shall ye move, and mortal be thy parts.'

And so beside the road they're bound to stand,
Each man of stone, stone sword in stony hand,
And we, the peris, we must mourn forever,
And bear a punishment that endeth never."

* * *

When Harmony finished, her sisters gravely applauded. By way of further explanation for Mustapha and Elcoloq, she added, "Of course that was long ago, even before the days of the Older Empire. When the father of Queen Nahrit sat the throne of power, the sands of the desert had already worn down the men of stone a considerable way. But never can the sands efface their human features. I wonder why?"

"It is a sorry fate to bear," said Mustapha, laying his hand on one of them, "but not an endless one."

"Endless! As our own fate is endless! Isn't it?" asked Pearl. She had commenced her utterance in a melting tone of sorrow, but the mood broke when she arrived at the inevitable question with which the peris invariably concluded everything they said.

"Why do the peris speak thus, ever ending in a question?" asked Mustapha. He thought it made them sound silly, but diplomatically kept his opinion to himself.

"Some say that it is mere habit," Wisdom replied. "Others suggest that it is part of the king's punishment. It may serve as a reminder to us that if we had questioned the evil chancellor more carefully in those days, we should not be in our predicament now. It also robs us of dignity. Years and years have passed since that lost age. My sisters and I, being immortal, were all present at the chancellor's unhappy instigation to rebellion. I suppose we ought to remember if we always end everything we say with a question.

"I myself have performed numerous experiments on the subject. While I find this phenomenon widespread among my sisters, to the point where linguistic studies end and epidemiology begins, I have also discovered that I am strangely immune to this affliction. I cannot help it if my sisters are careless in their speech patterns. It is a harmless aberration. I expected as much of them, since they are all named to be tutelary spirits of tangibles, or phenomena that are tangible-related. Ecstasy, for example, can only be expressed by tangible agents. Laughter also proceeds from a tangible source and is prompted by the tangible stimuli of the senses. Wisdom, on the other hand, is by far that most intangible thing in the earth, the seas, or the heavens. No wonder, then, say I, that I alone am untouched by the barbaric vocal quirks of peridom in general and my sisters in particular. Besides, they are all bubbleheads. Don't you agree?"

Fortunately for Wisdom's dignity, her inescapable final question was smothered by the Pomegranate's frightened cry. "It grows late, and we are not yet there, are we?"

"No, so we had better be going, oughtn't we?" said Wildrose.

The peri procession, with Mustapha and Elcoloq in their midst, proceeded along the hidden royal highway, under the stony gaze of the garnet captives.

Chapter XIV

PUTTING ON THE DOG

Who can know time in the heart of the desert? The sun fades, the sun rises, the sun hangs suspended above the iron sky for thrice eternity, the sun is gone. Night comes shyly on. She scarcely dares to touch the burning hands of the desert with the cooling kiss of darkness. Then the night flees, afraid. Sometimes there·are cool, distant stars in the heavens. Sometimes the stars tread upon the earth with the feet of women.

Mustapha and Elcoloq could not know how far they had traveled or what time of day it was. The splendor of the peris glowed brilliantly all around them, competing with the sun and slaying the kindly darkness of night. However, the peris knew enough about mortals to stop their march occasionally and look after their captives' needs.

It was not a boring journey. Peris love questions, being forced to use them all the time, and they love inquisitive mortals. Mustapha and Elcoloq quickly caught on to this quirk and exploited it.

"Why do we not fly anymore?" asked the dog.

"Aye, why do we walk for so long?" put in Mustapha.

"What charming thoughts!" said Laughter. "We must come on foot before the one we serve, to show our submission. Isn't that right, Wildrose?"

"Yes, Laughter," said her sister. "We walk far because she whom we serve can see far. She would punish us if we did not come on foot before her, not just into her palace but all the way along her royal road. Or is it highway?"

"Are we nearly there?" asked Mustapha.

"Behold, mortal!" declaimed Wisdom. "What do you think of that?" And with her sword of light, Wisdom pointed to the miracle that arose before them out of the desert.

The paving of the royal highway lurched suddenly free of the sands and they trod upon rich slabs of marble and porphyry, still guarded by the garnet watchmen. Mustapha gaped at the marvel before him. It was a palace, but a palace beyond dreams and reason. The royal highway divided itself to bypass the sumptuous parklands that stretched away in front of them. A golden fence surrounded lush greenery and velvet lawns.

The peris opened a little gate in the golden fence and led their captives to the castle by way of a shortcut through the park. Few trees were there, but flowering bushes grew in profusion. Through the fragrant branches Mustapha and El-coloq could still see the royal highway, now flanked by stone colossi, to either side of the park. To the left were titanic semblances of men, all strong, cold-featured, arrogant. To the right stood images of beautiful women, as alike as sisters. Statues challenged the heavens in their height and defied the earth in their expression. Yet beneath the beauty and the boldness, all wore a look of hidden trembling.

In the center of the park was a pool, a pool as deep as dreaming, yet so clear that Mustapha and Elcoloq could see to the very bottom. Strange things they beheld there: plants that appeared to have turned to rosy stone, plants that looked like the magnificent antlers of stags, tender green weeds that drifted languidly in the verdant depths, and exotic willowy fishes with long golden veils spread out behind them. Once, for an instant, Mustapha thought he also saw in the emerald waters a being that was spoken of in tales, a fish with the face of a mortal woman. The peris hurried him along before he could steal a second look.

They left the first park and crossed a narrow roadway of crushed pink stone, coming to a second wondrous garden. Here were no trees, no bushes in blossom, but only finely kept stretches of greensward and low borders of fragrant herbs, all made sweet with fragile flowers. In the center of this place danced a silver fountain, very like the wishing fountains Mustapha had seen in his travels. He stole a peep over the edge of the basin, just to see if anyone had tossed a copper in and made a wish. In place of coins he saw rubies and sapphires and diamonds and emeralds, each too large for a man to wear comfortably on a ring. If this was the accepted coin of the wishing fountain, thought Mustapha, what wishes it must grant!

At the end of this park was a wall of poplars with a high gate set in it all of silver, as huge as the doors of a castle. Before this barrier the peris stopped. They bustled about, chattering as nervously as a group of frightened sparrows, then at last moved into formal marching order: Two by two, with eight in front of Mustapha and Elcoloq and eight behind. Bliss, standing at the head of the assembled ranks, waited until another peri tied gossamer leads around the necks of Mustapha and Elcoloq and took up a position at their side. When everyone was arranged to her satisfaction, Bliss spoke.

"Open, we beg"—she addressed the silver gates—"in the name of she who rules us all wisely and well and with infinite beauty. All hail the august and lovely personage of Queen Nahrit!" And for once a peri didn't end her speech with a question. The massive gates swung back of their own power and permitted Mustapha his first view of the marvel to end all marvels, the dwelling-place of Queen Nahrit of the Older Empire.

A soaring flight of marble stairs ascended before him like a flood of moonlight, flanked on each side by an enthroned colossus of rosy stone. To the left Mustapha saw the shining figure of a queen, wearing a crown of gold and swathed in golden tissue. He recognized in her features the woman that Ayree had described to him in the distant icy halls of Castle Snowglimmer. In her crown glittered the banded glory of the tiger's-eye. The other statue was of a man, more handsome than any Mustapha had ever seen. It reminded him a little of his father; the merchant had been striking in his youth. Mustapha touched his father's miniature portrait, which he still bore near his heart despite all his journeys and adventures.

Between the titan figures the stairs led up to double doors of bronze chased with gold and silver. The palace itself looked to be made of gold. "Impossible," Mustapha muttered. "How could it stand? Gold is too soft to support such a huge edifice. It must be stone overlaid with gold, or the work of magic."

In shape the palace was like a half-finished pyramid, surmounted with a flat roof of whitest marble. This snowy crown was thick and wide, and well displayed the extensively carved friezes, with their scenes of hunts, battles, loves, and triumphs.

Mustapha and Elcoloq climbed the stairs and entered the golden hall in wonder. No one told them to keep silent, but in its grandeur the edifice itself demanded voiceless homage. Mustapha recovered just as they passed through the brazen portals and said, "Never did I think to come within the palace of Queen Nahrit! Never in my life nor in my dreams!"

"Silly motal," giggled Laughter, who held their leash. "This is not worthy to be so much as the servants' quarters of the palace of Queen Nahrit. Alas, the palace is gone from the earth, eaten by the ages, and this poor humble shelter is but Queen Nahrit's tomb. We sometimes call it her palace among ourselves to recall the olden times. Isn't that sad?" The procession entered the tomb, and the huge gates swung closed behind them.

They were in a high-roofed hall, the walls golden and decorated with the scarlet paintings Ayree had spoken of, the ceiling supported by jade pillars. It was a place of barbaric splendor, and for all his southern upbringing, Mustapha missed Ayree, his sweet sisters, and the coolly subtle design of Castle Snowglimmer.

At the end of the hall, in a flickering darkness that even a myriad of scented torches couldn't banish, there sat a woman on a jeweled throne. She was the image of the female colossus of the outer stairs, but she lived, she glowed with animated beauty. Before her the peris bowed in worship.

"Hail, O Chosen One!" said Bliss. "We bring before thee these two creatures that we found upon the desert. Speak, that we may know and do the work of Queen Nahrit!"

The woman answered in a voice almost as melodious as that of the peris. "Let them be lodged well. The royal will shall be known later. I shall speak with them myself. You have done well. You may go." She wore a diadem on her head and held a golden wand in her hand. She reached out with the wand and the peris shrank to the size of butterflies. They formed a living carpet beneath the feet of Mustapha and Elcoloq. As the travelers stood bewildered, the peris levitated them and bore them from the presence chamber through a little door hidden in the shadows.

They glided through long corridors feebly lit by lonely torches, coming at last to a richly appointed room furnished with a luxurious bed, soft divans, fine inlaid chairs and tables, and deep cushions entirely to Elcoloq's liking. A long table lay against one wall, freighted with food and drink. Behind an azure damask curtain a bathing pool beckoned. Into this paradise the peris set Mustapha and his dog, then resumed the size of mortal women.

"These are your quarters," said Hyacinth. "Do you like them?"

"Very much, gracious lady," said Mustapha. "Shall it be our pleasure to see you and your fair sisters again?"

"Perhaps," Hyacinth said absently. "If Her Majesty will allow it. We rather like you. Are you pleased?"

"I am delighted," replied Mustapha, touching his brow with both hands in the sign meaning that he was their humble servant. The peris giggled and hid their faces. In a great flutter they left the room, shutting the door behind them. It closed with an ominous click.

Elcoloq sniffed at it. "Locked," he announced.

"How can you tell by smelling it whether or not it is locked?" asked Mustapha. He tried the door and found Elcoloq's judgment to be correct.

"I can tell," said Elcoloq.

Nor did the room have any windows. Torches and braziers provided the only light. "It is to be expected," reasoned Mustapha. "Who ever heard of placing windows in a tomb?"

But Elcoloq was no longer listening. He leaped upon the groaning table as lightly as a cat and helped himself to a leg of mutton. Mustapha joined him at the feast, pouring water for them both. Seductive flasks of wine—white, red, pink, and green—stood invitingly, but a clear head was worth more to Mustapha now than any wine, were it made by the hands of the peris themselves.

At last Mustapha stretched out on a sheepskin-covered divan. "I find the beauty of Queen Nahrit more fabulous than anything I could have imagined," he remarked to Elcoloq. "That she yet lives, when the Older Empire is reduced to dust, is a wonder. But why will she persist in hiding such loveliness as hers, even within so sumptuous a tomb? Surely she must command enough wealth to rebuild her true palace. She who commands the legion of the air, who rules the peris, should certainly have the means to do this. Why think you, Elcoloq, that she who is so fair, who sits so regally upon that throne, does not reveal herself to the dreaming world?"

"Because," said Elcoloq, "she is not Queen Nahrit."

Chapter XV

DOGGING HER FOOTSTEPS

"Elcoloq, you are mad!" Mustapha gasped. "Ayree himself described Queen Nahrit to us. This woman is she, as sure as I am Mustapha. Why should the peris kneel before her if she is not Queen Nahrit? How can you say she is not Queen Nahrit?"

"We do not know who it was that Ayree saw," said the sage animal. "As for the peris, they are immortal fools and mindless coquettes—sweet to see, but dangerous, being stupid. And did you not notice that row of statues outside the palace? If we accept only Ayree's description, any one of those women might be Queen Nahrit. I tell you, master, my nose can discern much, and I smelled nothing of royalty about that woman. There is even about her," he averred, "a distinct aroma of garlicked lamb stew."

"You shall beg the pardon of Her Majesty for that last remark!" Mustapha thundered indignantly. "How could such a wonder of loveliness subsist on more than honey and flower petals? Garlicked lamb stew indeed!"

Elcoloq said nothing, but his look of condescending patience could have enraged a saint.

Finally the dog replied, "If my nose did not lie about the locked door, how could it be mistaken about the more obvious fact of garlicked lamb stew? Let us be on our guard, master. I smell treachery here."

"Treachery? Saw you not the queen? A face of sweetness and kindness! The sadness in her eyes could only reflect a compassionate soul. Elcoloq, if she is as wise as she is fair, you will soon be a normal dog again. I envy you, who shall receive healing from those adorable hands."

"Master, I say that we should bide our time. The fur on my back rebels in this place. Trust anything but your eyes! Gorgeous the peris may be, yet they have done much evil. Through all the ages that they have lived, they have only learned to pinch and tug at leashes. I beg you, master, do not—"

Elcoloq never finished his plea. A chill wind swept through the windowless chamber, extinguishing the torches. In the blackness they heard the door crash open. Winds of lost places howled around their heads. Then the winds stopped wailing and from the shadows came the same sweet voice that they had heard earlier in the presence hall.

"O mortals!" it intoned. "I am Queen Nahrit, last ruler of the Older Empire. For years I have slept the sleep of your world here in my tomb, wishing not to be disturbed in my rest, in my slumbers. Now you come before me. Why? The final outpost of my vanished empire lies isolated on the great Desert of Thulain, a resort for my servants. They found you there and brought you to me. Tell me your purpose."

Mustapha peered into the dark, trying to see the speaker. Elcoloq trembled, his tail fast between his legs. "O most powerful queen!" Mustapha replied. "We are your humble slaves, come to behold your magnificence. It is rumored in the waking world that the beauty, mercy, kindness, and glory of Queen Nahrit did not perish with the Older Empire, but still lives on. My heart rejoices to discover that such sayings are true, and now I do earnestly beg of you to grant us a second sight of Your Majesty."

There was a hesitation in the dark before the voice spoke again. "You have already been before my sight in the presence hall. That must suffice. Speak now! Tell me who you are and your true purpose here! You did not wander the desert merely to learn if I were still alive. I am no fool, mortals."

Mustapha answered in a voice meant to charm women. "I am Mustapha; my dog is called Elcoloq. In happier days we traveled abroad as performers, but now our mission brings us before you. We are come, O most radiant queen, to ask you— *ow!*"

For no apparent reason, Elcoloq sank his teeth into his beloved master's ankle and refused to let go. A scuffle began in the pitch-black room. Mustapha's commands for the beast to release him went unheeded. As the two of them thrashed around, the noises of toppling braziers and crashing tableware added to the general hullaballoo.

"What is this?" The voice was indignant. "Let this unseemly behavior cease at once!"

"Believe me—*ow!*—Your Majesty— Let *go!*— I'm trying!" shouted Mustapha as he fell against yet another brazier, its coals still smoldering. "Aaaa! Elcoloq, let me go before you start a fire!"

The dog only growled in answer, and kept tussling until there came the sound of an exasperated snort, the slamming of a door, and the marvelous restoration of light to the room.

Mustapha and Elcoloq were sprawled amid a glorious shambles: Several of the divans were upset, the table was overturned, and a number of ripped cushions were yielding their feathers to the playful breezes. Elcoloq released Mustapha's ankle and sat back on his haunches, satisfied. Mustapha did not share the dog's contentment.

"Dog and Child of Dogs!" swore Mustapha, too furious to realize that this was no insult to Elcoloq. "What is the meaning of this? You have probably chewed my leg through to the very bone! Ungrateful beast! Was it for this that I brought you here?"

"Calmly, master, calmly," said the dog. "Look and you shall see that there is not even the mark of a single tooth on your august ankle. I had my purpose in what I did. Be guided by me, master, I beg of you."

"Guided? How guided? Guided to insult Queen Nahrit, when you do not even believe her to be Queen Nahrit? Oh, she will be very willing to heal you after this behavior, I am sure! Let me lay our purpose before her and be done with it. Let her give or withhold her help and then let us be gone. What is simpler? What guidance do I need in all this?"

"Behold, master, and tell me," said Elcoloq. With his paw, he offered a scrap of cloth to Mustapha. The cloth was scarlet brocade with the hint of silver embroidery; expensive but unremarkable. Mustapha took it and held it closer to his eyes for more careful inspection but suddenly dropped it and leaped away.

"What is it, master?" asked the dog, with a look that said he knew very well what it was.

"The smell!" replied Mustapha, in a voice trembling with horror. "It has been a long time, Elcoloq, since I first learned where such a smell may come from. When I was but a child, I met an ancient man who came wandering through our village. We gave him food, but I noticed how the serving girls would not stay near him long, how they would hold scented cloths before their noses in his presence. I was a curious child. I drew close to see what it was about him that was so repugnant. He was not an ugly old man or deformed in any way. And then, as I came nigh, that smell met my nostrils and I, too, drew away.

"The old man caught me at it. I feared he would tell my father and I would be punished for treating a guest rudely. He only laughed, that old gentleman, and told me that he doubted I should ever again smell such a scent as that. He had worked for forty long years as public executioner of his little city, charged not only with killing convicted felons but with finding them burial by his own hand also. 'It is the smell of long years spent holding the hand of death, little one,' he told me. He is dead himself, years ago. Yet now I perceive that same awful smell again on this cloth. Where did you get this?"

"In the dark," said the dog, "I smelled that very death-scent you speak of and traced it to its source. If you can sense the dreaming horror of that deathly perfume, think of how more acutely I can smell it! I tore that scrap from the robe that clothed the one who spoke to us in darkness. Aye, it was taken from the scarlet robe of Queen Nahrit."

"This cannot be so!" Mustapha protested. "You saw her yourself. She is as fresh as a blooming lotus. Death has never come near her. How can such a vision smell of death?"

"O foolish and well-loved master," said the dog, "because I did not take this from the robe of the queen we saw in the presence hall, but from the one who spoke to us in darkness."

Mustapha was silent for a long time, regarding the dog as if it had gone quite mad. Then he said, "Do you claim that the one who lately spoke to us is Queen Nahrit? Rather, perhaps she is the queen impostor. Is it not easier to counterfeit a voice than a beautiful face?"

"I know not," said the dog. "But I counsel secrecy until we do know, and until whoever speaks to us from the curtains of shadow will show herself to us. Tell her nothing of our true purpose here. It may be that I will need my powers of transformation more now than ever. There is more at stake than a bit of pickpocket work. This tomb reeks of treachery, new and old. Choose for the moment a false reason to seek out Queen Nahrit. Give us some time."

"A reason . . ." Mustapha pondered. The door opened as he mulled this thought over in his mind. It was Laughter, in the company of Bliss and Wildrose. They surveyed the ransacked chamber and sighed.

"Wouldn't you and your dog like to follow Bliss into the central courtyard?" suggested Laughter. "I think it would be easier for us to tidy up if you were out of the way, don't you?"

Mustapha bowed and followed the fair peri out of the room while her two sisters set about restoring some order. Bliss conducted them through many corridors until they emerged in a square court open to the sky. A shallow golden fountain supported by four golden bulls bubbled in the center of the mosaic pavement. The gilded walls of Queen Nahrit's tomb rose up high around them, shading the court deliciously from the desert sun. Benches of black marble lined the walls, and on one of these Mustapha sat, Elcoloq at his feet, enjoying the fresh air.

"What an adorable place!" sighed Mustapha.

"It is the heart of Queen Nahrit's tomb, the very center," said Bliss. "Do you see that fountain? Between the hind legs of the bulls is an iron box that contains the heart of Lord Oran, wrapped in linen and set with spices. Oh, dear! I really should go back to my sisters and help them tidy up. Will you excuse me?" She fluttered away.

As Mustapha sat there, the silence broken only by the plashing of the fountain, he was suddenly amazed to hear the soft sound of human weeping high above his head. He would have looked up, but the restraining jaws of Elcoloq prevented him, grabbing hold of his robe. In the lowest of whispers the dog said, "Hush! Wait and listen and learn." So Mustapha waited.

The weeping went on. Then there was a pause, after which the tears changed to the sound of a woman lamenting.

Between trembling sobs and dolorous sighs she complained, "Was anyone ever so unfortunate as I? How much longer must I suffer my captivity? My nineteenth birthday sets me free, they say. That shall soon come. Then what shall become of me? The cruel ones tell me nothing! May the day I was sold be a dark day forevermore!"

A second voice, tinkling like silver bells beyond the stars, interrupted the first one. "You are wanted below," it said. "Do not let her wait long upon your coming, will you?"

"No," answered the first voice in most pathetic sweetness. "I will go to her even now." There was silence again in the courtyard.

"I have heard that voice before," said Mustapha.

"Of course you have. It was one of the peris," said the dog.

"Nay, but the other voice, the first voice. I have heard it before, only moments since."

"Doubtless it was she who spoke to us in the darkened room," suggested Elcoloq. "It is the voice of one who seeks not to be seen."

"Nay," Mustapha said again. "The speaker in shadow had a voice as sweet, but not as gentle. For all of its melody, that voice was one of command, of a strong will, and with little room for kindness. But the voice we just heard belongs to some poor mortal servant of the queen. It speaks of mortal knowledge and suffering. My heart can tell me more things than your nose tells you, my friend."

"What mortal could hover above our heads?" asked the dog. "The voice came from above, from the very air and sky, like the voices of peris. Can mortals fly?"

"O infinitely dear and foolish dog," Mustapha said with a distinctly patronizing air. "Look there. A balcony encircles this courtyard, just above us. She did indeed walk over our heads, but on marble, not on air. We must find her, Elcoloq. We must help her. I fear that we mortal beings are pitifully few in this place of mystery. And I have heard her speak before now, I know it!"

"In a dream, perhaps"—Elcoloq shrugged—"for would it not—" He stopped, for the peris had returned to conduct them back to their room. Mustapha courteously entreated them to allow his dog to enjoy the freedom of the courtyard for just a little while longer.

"No, by no means," said Laughter. "How can we allow it?"

"But he could find my room again with ease, lady," said Mustapha.

"By no means," echoed Bliss. "The queen desires to see you both. What if he became lost?"

"So that is settled," said Wildrose. "Won't you come along like a good dog?" She reached for Elcoloq.

With eloquence of gesture, Elcoloq trotted up to the portal and lifted his leg against the creamy marble pillar. The peris drew back in dismay. Each time they tried to coax him within doors, he made as if to repeat the gesture.

"Ladies," said Mustapha to the perplexed peris, "it would seem that my dog has need of exercise and the freedom of other functions better suited to the courtyard than the bed-chamber . . . unless you would like to clean the room again?"

The peris showed no great eagerness to do that. Elcoloq was left at liberty in the courtyard and the corridors. The peris charged him severely to return to his master's room as soon as he might have satisfied nature sufficiently.

Once alone in the courtyard, Elcoloq sniffed around the walls and fountain dutifully, glancing slyly out of the corner of his eye to see if anyone was watching. Then, satisfied that he was indeed alone and unwatched, he enjoyed a long laugh.

"O dearest and most innocent of masters!" he chuckled to himself. "And did you think that you really were the one who showed the balcony to me? And did you think that I did not know whose voice it was we heard lamenting from that balcony? But you are human, my dear master. You must always be allowed to believe that your ideas are all your own. May it be the will of the gods that your purblind human nature will not prevent our escape from this place. By my fangs and fur, this is truly a place of evil, a place of death."

Elcoloq gave a final glance about the deserted courtyard where the four golden bulls stood watch over the heart of Oran and the fountain plashed a melancholy melody. Then he plunged swiftly into the maze of corridors within the tomb of Queen Nahrit. What he searched for, he alone knew.

Chapter XVI

DOG-EARED

The tomb of Queen Nahrit might have been a palace for all its winding corridors, lavish decoration, and solemn grandeur. But for all the shadows and empty hallways Elcoloq encountered, it was a tomb indeed. The corridors were filled with hollow echoes, the decorations obscured by a thin film of dust, and the grandeur of the place was that of a dead march played upon a muffled drum.

The sharp scrabbling sounds that Elcoloq's nails made on the black marble floors returned to his ears as loud as any thunder, but no one seemed to notice him in his wanderings. He followed a scent, a scent he had caught and held before, in the presence hall, and then again in the courtyard. Now, through all the twists and turns, the roamings and ramblings of the darksome halls within the tomb of Queen Nahrit, Elcoloq followed the scent of a homely lamb stew, liberally laced with garlic.

Laughter held wide the door to Mustapha's room, ushered him inside, and locked it fast behind him. Fresh food and drink graced the table, and Wildrose had added a bowl of flowers. Yet it did not cease to be a prison, no matter how many flowers there might be. Mustapha sat on the divan and reflected on all he had seen and heard since entering the realm of Queen Nahrit. Perhaps Elcoloq had been right to advise caution. Caution, he thought, but how should he proceed?

He reached inside his robe and took out the small leather pouch that guarded his chiefest treasures, his only relics of home. No hunger was too sharp to make him part with either one. The necklace spilled glimmering into his out-stretched palm, twined lovingly about the miniature of his father. Mustapha sighed.

It was as if that sigh extinguished all the torches that lit the room. Once more he found himself enveloped in total darkness and heard again the voice of an unseen speaker from out of the shadows.

"O stranger!" said the voice. "Are you now prepared to speak before me and tell me your true purpose in my lands?"

"Most beautiful of queens," said Mustapha, "I am." He bowed low in the direction of the voice. If the peris feared the far-seeing vision of Queen Nahrit enough to come on foot for miles to her presence, Mustapha suspected that she would also possess enchantments to pierce the dark. Whether she could see his gesture of respect or not, he performed it in any case.

"You are courteous, at least," said the voice. Mustapha thanked the gods who had prompted him to bow to shadows. "Speak. I listen."

"Radiant Dawn of the World," said Mustapha, "I come before your glory as—as a humble messenger."

"A messenger? What message do you bring me? Say on! Why do you hesitate?"

Mustapha clenched his fists and wished that Elcoloq were there. The dog was better at improvising than his master. In all their years together it had been so. Mustapha racked his imagination for some message that would both gratify the unseen one and buy them some more time. The stones of his mother's necklace felt cold as ice against his sweating palm, and the wintry feeling gave him a sudden thought.

"My name is Mustapha; my unworthy beast is named Elcoloq," he said. "We are but the vassals of one whose glory and majesty dare to rival your own. Our master—whose bounty be praised—is powerful in the hidden arts. Through the channels of the air he heard a rumor that the legendary Queen Nahrit still lived. How could he believe such whispers? The air-spirits are always weaving truth and falsehood. My master dared not believe it. 'O Mustapha!' he cried. 'I have long despaired of finding any queen worthy to be my bride. I have read the tales of the Older Empire. I have read of Queen Nahrit, but men say she is no more. Oh, if she only lived, how blessed would I be! I will have no other than Queen Nahrit for my chosen bride!' Then he would weep. Think of his bliss when he first heard that you might still walk the earth!" Mustapha paused.

"Yes, yes!" the voice cried sharply, impatiently. "Go on, Mustapha! Go on, I say!"

Her eagerness to hear more of his story reassured Mustapha that the bait had been well taken. Knowing that the speaker in shadow could see through darkness, Mustapha did not allow himself to smile. Instead he said, "Go on? But that is all, Your Majesty. My master would marry you, if you are willing. I have no more to say."

"But his name, Mustapha!" urged the voice. "You do not tell me your master's name! You are a careless servant indeed."

Mustapha inclined his head slightly and replied, "Forgive me, Beacon of the Southern Skies. The name of my master, certainly. The all-gracious, the bountiful, the kind master that I serve is called Ayree."

"Ayree! Ayree the warlock prince?" The voice was ravished with delight. Mustapha gave thanks to the icy touch of his mother's necklace that had recalled Castle Snowglimmer and its young lord. The speaker in shadow had heard of Ayree and seemed more than pleased with Mustapha's proposal.

"Dare I hope," entreated a very humble Mustapha, "that the Flower of All Graces knows my unworthy master?"

"Who does not know Ayree?" answered the voice, softer now. "Know, mortal, that he and I are of one blood and one power. If the powers of enchantment did not run in my veins, how could you still face me, whose empire fell in days before you were even a thought?" The voice became quite tender as it continued, saying, "Ayree, most powerful of mages, and most handsome! Not since the days when I yet ruled my empire from the lost palace have I heard of a man so handsome as Ayree. Not even he whom my heart loved, my lost one, my Oran, could rival Ayree, child of the stars!" There were tears in the voice now, and silence followed.

Mustapha inquired timidly, "Most Ravishing of Women, we of the world beyond your lands have heard much of your power and your beauty, but never of any man that you loved. Who was this Oran?"

"Oran, mortal?" The voice was indignant. "You have not heard of Oran? Do they no longer sing of him—of his courage, of his beauty? Do you not know that it was his death alone that caused the Older Empire to crumble and be lost upon the desert sands? Know you none of this?"

"Indeed, Majestic One, nothing."

There was a long silence before the voice spoke again. "I pity you, Mustapha. Your world has lost much in losing the story of Oran. Nor can you hope to find it again, for my heart would break if I had to tell it to you. Let this suffice: I loved him and did not speak of love in time; he died, not knowing of my love. For that reason I have bided here, within this tomb, watching the sorry panoply of earth pass by me to their silent graves. My heart is dead, though nothing else of me has changed. Time does not touch me, Mustapha. That is my power. In vain I searched your dreaming cities for one with a power beyond mine, a power to bring my heart to life again. I sought, but I found nothing—nothing, until the day I first heard of your master, Ayree. Then, Mustapha, in the shrunken darkness of my heart I thought I felt new life. I can never love again as I loved Oran, but perhaps I can feel a lesser love."

"Angelic One, why did you not speak to my master before this?" asked Mustapha.

"Speak to him? I would have. I yearned to tell him that I lived and that I hoped to love him. But Ayree's throne lies beyond the scope of my power. The winds of the north freeze and shatter my enchantments. I had to wait and hope that he would learn by his most potent arts that I lived. Now behold, Mustapha! It has happened! The union of myself and Ayree is meant to be!" the voice exulted. "At last, at last I have found one worthy to be my mate, to raise up again the Older Empire from the dust of dreams and legends! Again I shall hold sway upon the earth, and mortal men shall once more tremble before my rule! I shall show my lord Ayree what it means to govern, what pleasures he may have, how delicious it is to know that there is no law but my desire. And you, Mustapha, shall be chief overseer of our slaves when we have again established our throne. This shall be your reward."

"Queen of Delight," ventured Mustapha, "I thank you,

but as I was once uncomfortably close to being a slave myself, I think I would rather not—"

"Fool!" Thunder filled the darkened room. "Do you know nothing of my empire? I shall not enslave those who oversee the slaves for me! But I shall have need of *many* slaves before my halls and palaces are rebuilt to my satisfaction."

Mustapha said nothing, feeling a hard knot of fear at his heart.

"Well?" the voice demanded.

"Your Majesty is gracious," he managed to say.

The unseen one seemed satisfied, for she said, "And did my lord Ayree send you with no further message?"

"Nay, Exalted One."

"What? No token of his love, but only words?" She was plainly irritated. That was logical, Mustapha realized. Surely one as greedy for slaves, lands, and power as was this invisible presence would also be greedy for smaller gifts. Sadly Mustapha realized what he had to do.

"Forgive me, Pearl of All Pearls! I almost forgot." And he extended his mother's necklace into the darkness. "A humble offering of love." The flesh of his hand shuddered with cold as another hand, small and icy, took the necklace from him. He imagined himself again in the hut of the snow-beast, with a cold more terrible than death around him. Truly, the smell of ageless death itself seemed to emanate from the touch of that hand. Mustapha almost reeled away at the charnel stench of it.

"It is a beautiful gift and worthy of the sender," said the voice. In the dark Mustapha heard the pendant gems of the necklace clicking one against the other, sounding as cold as the scales of a snake over ivory tiles.

"If you are pleased with my master's gift," said Mustapha, "perhaps you will inform your mistress of it at once, that she may give her answer to Ayree's proposal."

"Mistress!" Lightning crackled with deadly chill across the blackened chamber. "Mistress, say you? Queen Nahrit has no mistress! You will bring destruction upon yourself with these brainless pratings!"

"Indeed, indeed," said Mustapha, his voice humble but his heart determined to force this unseen one to reveal herself, "I never said that Queen Nahrit had mistress or master in the world. I only asked you to go and inform the queen, your mistress, of my words."

"I *am* the queen! Even now you called me 'Majesty'! Have you gone mad?"

"Sweetheart, I play the game that pleases you. High rulers often speak through servants. If you are the queen, why do you hide the glorious face that you let me see so freely in the presence hall? I think—"

"I am the queen, dog!"

Fire filled the room. Fire and the light of fire licked upward to the ceiling. Cold fire shone fiercely from the tall fury of a woman who stood revealed before Mustapha. It was the face he had seen in the presence hall. The tawny hair, the golden skin, the topaz eyes spoke of her identity. On her head she wore the crown of tiger's-eye; in her hand she bore the golden wand.

It is she, thought Mustapha. Elcoloq was wrong, with his tales of lamb stew. And yet, I doubt her. There is something wrong. Her hair, her face, her dress are all the same, but what does that matter? There are things beyond the portals of our senses that speak to us and tell us that they lie, our senses lie. Our hearts tell us, or our souls. Who can name the force that works such wonders? This is not the lady of the presence hall. By smell alone a simple beast can find her cub out of a thousand others. A man may find the love of his childhood years changed by age, and still know her. This is not the woman of the presence hall. Ah, but without doubt this is the living Queen Nahrit.

Prudently, in the very moment of this realization, Mustapha fell groveling to the floor at the dainty, pointed feet of the raging queen. "Forgive! Forgive, O Beneficent One, the evil words of my stupid tongue! Forgive, but tell me, how was I to know that you were not indeed your own servant sent to test me? My master bade me be cautious. In the dark, how was I to know?"

His words and his complete obeisance mollified the queen somewhat. The flames subsided, leaving her surrounded with an icy golden aura that lit but did not warm the room.

"You speak well," she said. "Arise. You are forgiven." She motioned him toward a divan. "We will speak of your master and my future lord, Ayree, now," she declared.

Chapter XVII

THE DOGS OF WAR

Elcoloq lost the scent a few times as he trotted briskly along the corridors. This was not always his fault, for the peris crisscrossed the trail he followed and obscured it with the flowery exhalation of their wings.

He avoided them easily. Their scent betrayed them, and their constant jabbering. In groups of twos and threes they roamed the tomb, attending to this or that, constantly gossiping. They paid no attention to a small shadow, huddled against a wall or pressed into a corner. They passed him by, and Elcoloq resumed his search.

He knew that it would end at a door: a closed door. And so it did. He left the mazy corridors of the first level, climbed a winding stair of porphyry, and sauntered down a short hall that had a floor patterned in gay mosaics. At last he found the expected door, silver set with panels of lapis lazuli that had been carved in low relief. He had expected a door, but not such a door, and certainly he had not expected it to be left unlocked. When he stood on his hindpaws to examine the carvings, he gave it a gentle push with his forepaws. It swung smoothly away from him, and he tumbled clumsily into the room beyond.

A girl was there, a lovely girl. She had laid aside the crown of tiger's-eye and the golden wand. She had put off her robes of glory and sat by the tiny window-slit in a simple wrap of worn white cotton, yet still she was lovely. Not even the traces of recent tears, or eyes reddened by weeping, could make her beauty less. When she saw Elcoloq, she screamed and fell to her knees.

"No! Oh, no, not this way! Oh, please, please, Your Majesty, only a little more time! Just a little more!" She hid her face in her hands and babbled something too low for Elcoloq to distinguish. She looked up at him for a moment, then hid her face once more.

He drew closer, puzzled. She peeped at him between her fingers and sprang away, until she stood trembling against the far wall, her eyes mirrors of terror. The fear he saw there was too much for Elcoloq to bear. He would have licked her feet if she would have let him come near.

"What do you fear? I won't harm you," he said. He wagged his tail, recalling that she had never heard him speak. For someone in her state, a talking dog might be too much to stand and still keep sane. He hoped a wagging tail was ordinary enough to calm her.

She relaxed somewhat at his words, but she was obviously still on guard. She came away from the wall and extended one hand tentatively. He licked it gently and placed his head beneath it, still wagging his tail.

"I remember you," she said. "The peris brought you and the man before me in the presence hall. I thought you were prisoners until I saw you come here by yourself. If you have the freedom of this place, you must be one of her creatures. The audience was one of her ruses. Who are you?"

"I am your friend," said Elcoloq, "and no one's creature."

"A friend? A friend for me, who has none? This is her final cruelty. Let me be deceived into thinking I have a friend only to have you spring upon me in the night and end my life when she commands it."

"I don't know what you mean," said Elcoloq. "I offer you friendship, not treachery. Why are you so suspicious? It may be only a dog's friendship, but it is better than none. I have followed your scent to this room, I have heard your tears in the courtyard, I have seen you in the presence hall, and I know that you are no queen. Well, I am no dog fit for royalty, either. Can you want or hope for more? Let me help you."

The girl allowed Elcoloq to snuggle beneath her arm. She stroked his fur, but still there was no trust in her golden eyes. "Where have you come from?" she asked. "I would guess that you come from the stars. There is no other place— unless you were born of her enchantments."

"Not so. My master and I come from Vair, beyond the mountains."

"Mountains? What are mountains? What is Vair? You are a strange creature. There is only the sand and the stars. My parents had a tent upon the sand. This place is set about with sand. From the stars come her evil servants and her power. There is nothing else."

"Where I come from," said Elcoloq, "many men say that there are no such things as peris, merely because they have never seen any."

The girl sighed. "I see the truth of what you say. Pay me no mind. I must sound senseless to you."

"You are a captive, poor child," Elcoloq sympathized. "But do not fear. I swear to you by my four paws and by the nose that led me here, a day shall come when I shall show you mountains."

The girl threw herself on Elcoloq and began to weep into his fur, hugging him tightly. He licked her face and let her weep for a while. "Dear, good beast! There is so much kindness in your voice that I must believe that you are not one of her wicked creations! I have lived here all my life and I recognize something new in you. You are my friend, dear one. But waste not your love and your sweet promises on one who is so soon to die!"

"You are young and healthy," said Elcoloq. "Why should you die?"

The girl laughed bitterly. "Come, friend," she said. "I will show you something to make you wise." She arose and guided him out through the paneled door, a few yards down the dimly lit hall, and into another room illuminated by an immense black chandelier ablaze with candles.

Elcoloq examined the room, so different from all the others he had seen. It was octagonal in shape, with one wall taken by the doorway and the other seven trimly fitted out with tier after tier of shelves. Every available inch of space on those shelves was taken up with slender wooden boxes. The girl reached up for one of these, a box covered with deep blue lacquer, and showed Elcoloq its contents: four tightly rolled parchment scrolls, tagged and tasseled.

"This is the queen's lesser library," said the girl. "Here she keeps all scrolls that do not deal with magic. She has a remarkable collection. On that shelf are scrolls of poetry;

there stand collections of tales that are now lost to the world; and there you may see songs that were written by blind Harmaz. And this," she said, indicating the shelf from which she had removed the box, "is history."

"You are permitted in this room?" asked Elcoloq.

"Certainly. What harm can it do? Although there was a time, when I was younger, that I was forbidden to enter here. Her Majesty had learned something concerning one of the scrolls. I remember it distinctly. She would vanish from our company from time to time and return with a strange new knowledge. Once she returned in a nervous state; very confused and desperate she looked. She banned us all from the lesser library, and we heard her rummaging through the scroll boxes like a madwoman. When she emerged, she carried a single scroll in her hand. She was calmer, but her looks were still confused.

"'What can he want with this?' I heard her say. 'What use is it to anyone? But he ordered me to hide it, and I owe him too much to disobey. Let it be so.' Then she ordered the peris to rearrange the scrolls. She had scattered them across the floor in her search for that one."

"Why was it so important?"

"We never learned. Her Majesty's whim, I think. I know the scrolls well. It came from the shelves devoted to the romances of the Older Empire. I think that Lord Oran figured in it, but he appears in all the histories and epics of that time. Now let me show you the scroll that will explain all to you."

The girl removed one scroll from the box and unrolled it. Elcoloq gave a passing sniff to the spidery alien characters, then said, "Mistress, I cannot read."

"No? But you speak!"

"I am a talking dog, nothing more. Enlighten me."

"This is the history of the fall of the Older Empire," said the girl, tracing out the lines with her finger. "It was written by Queen Nahrit herself, in the centuries of leisure that she spent within this tomb. It was in those final days of the Older Empire that a hope arose among the people, a hope of a hero to save them. The astrologers of the royal court predicted his coming, and all prayed to live until that day. Queen Nahrit herself ascended the throne before reports came to her of the young hero, Oran. He was brought into her presence.

"She writes here that she loved him with all her heart, but he died. No mention is made of how that happened. The Older Empire, which he might have saved, began to crumble, and the people murmured that Queen Nahrit herself was to blame for Oran's death. They spoke of overthrowing her, of choosing a king, of governing themselves, of many things. They even spoke of killing her.

"Queen Nahrit had become wise in the few years of her reign. She sent out false reports that she was dead. On a litter of gold overlaid with gems, Queen Nahrit was borne into her tomb. Many of the people rejoiced.

"Their joy was short. The Older Empire fell soon after. The subjects and the slaves of Queen Nahrit wandered from their ruined cities. The desert claimed the lands of the Older Empire, where all men thought that Queen Nahrit lay wrapped in dreamless death.

"Then men in other lands heard rumors, the tales of seers and mages, concerning Queen Nahrit. They said that she had not died, that she lived on. Some of them had seen her in visions. She lived in her tomb, amidst the massed wealth of her fallen citadel, awaiting the hero who would brave the desert to win her hand. Many men went forth, lured by her fabled beauty and her wealth. None returned.

"New tales arose: Queen Nahrit had transformed herself into a monster and lay curled around the outside of her tomb, a giant fire-worm, waiting to devour any man who came to steal her treasure. Many men set forth to slay the beast. None returned.

"Other tales were told. Sorcerers in dim caves claimed they saw her in their crystals. She was no fire-worm, but still as lovely as she had ever been. From time to time she appeared to trouble the dreams of men, always with a look of anguish on her face. It was said that she was a prisoner of demons and awaited the man who would slay the friends and set her free. The lost glory of the Older Empire would then return to the dry and dreamless earth. Again men went forth to save the captive queen. Again not one returned.

"That is what she writes. Now I will tell you the truth, good dog. It is part of all the legends, and it is all of none.

Queen Nahrit lives, more cruel than any demon, more fierce than any fire-worm. From her false death she summoned the peris to serve her. By forbidden magic she secured a life so long that it was almost eternal. But all her spells could never obtain the gift of endless youth.

"She sent out the peris to fetch her a human girl on the day she first saw that age was claiming her beauty. The girl was always young and fair, her looks as close to those of the queen as possible. It was the girl that walked among the dreams and the crystals of the sorcerers. It was the girl they found, those men who came here seeking the queen and her treasure. She lured those few unfortunates to their deaths, and when she grew too old to resemble her mistress any longer, the girl was also put to death."

"You are that girl," said Elcoloq solemnly. "But where does she obtain those poor girls who resemble her? Where did you come from?"

The girl smiled sadly. "I have the consolation of one thought," she said. "I am the last girl she shall ever have to enslave for such a wicked design. I was the child of desert wanderers, a girl-child and worthless. Imagine my parents when the splendor of the queen's peri messenger shone before them and offered them gold for a worthless babe. That is how I came here. In those days there were many girls in this place. One impersonated the queen; one a little younger than she was in training. There was one younger still, and then myself. Those three raised me, loved me, and left me when it came their time to die. Now I am alone. Soon I will follow them."

"You are alone no longer," Elcoloq said staunchly. "We will save you. My master is called Mustapha. But what is your name?"

The girl laughed. "I have none. Call me Nahrit, if you like. I will not need a name for long."

Elcoloq snorted. "You'll need one when we return to Vair. We shall deliver you, and any other mortals in this tomb."

"I am the last," repeated the girl. "Shortly after my arrival, I saw a change come over the queen. You know those times I spoke of when she vanishes?" Elcoloq nodded. "Well, when I was small I saw her return from one such retreat, and she was no longer old. Her face rivaled that of the girl who took her place in the dreams of men. She would still age, but each time she did, she left us and came back young again. And each time she returned," sighed the girl, "one of my elder sisters would vanish, never to return again."

"I do not like this scent," said Elcoloq. "Never mind. You will vanish, but to Vair! I swear it!"

The girl stared at him for a moment, then hugged him and whispered, "I want to believe you! I *want* to see more of the world than sand and stars! But it will be so hard, so hard. Did you not see the row of statues as you entered the tomb? They are the effigies of the girls who came before me and the men who came in search of them—save two, the first two, of Queen Nahrit and Lord Oran. I fear the last two shall be me and your master."

"We'll see about that," said Elcoloq. "I shall bring my master to you soon, and we shall flee together. Be ready, and do not despair." He licked her hands in a courtly way and then slipped from the room.

The girl waited until the last of his swift footfalls ceased to echo in the queen's lesser library. She still held the unfurled scroll. "Fare you well," she said, in the manner of one accustomed to talking to herself. "I wish you well. I have read of the outer world, dear friend, and I have longed to see it. Perhaps now—"

The candles of the black chandelier grew smoky and flickered. The girl jerked her head up to stare at the perishing flames and was afraid, for she could feel no wind. The chandelier danced madly on its chain as if batted here and there by a giant cat's paw, and the floor shook beneath her feet. A sound of deep, humorless laughter swelled in her ears.

"'Perhaps'?" a voice deep as night mimicked her. "Does the slave speak of perhaps? Of friends? Of the outer world?" Again there came the laughter, like great empty wine barrels careening down a chute of stone.

In panic the girl ran for the library's open doorway, only to collide with a barrier she could feel without seeing. Her arms were seized by large, invisible hands, talons digging mercilessly into her flesh.

"You will tell me more of these dreams!" cried the voice. "You will sing of this for me, slave! Aye, you will make most interesting music!"

The air of the doorway darkened and began to take colossal shape before the girl's eyes. Hands the color of burned bone appeared, clutched around her arms. The claws that tipped the heavy fingers were as long and pearly as a peri's. Arms knotted with muscles, legs like the trunks of cypress trees, a torso almost too broad to pass through the doorway—all materialized. The girl tilted her head and screamed when she saw the hideous face that leered down at her from a height of seven feet. Yellow fangs and yellow eyes flashed before her, and a tongue as red as blood lolled from the twisted mouth.

"Ah, you did not expect me, did you?" roared the creature. "But you have heard of me, slave! I am the most faithful of our dear queen's servants, and the most feared. I am Rihman the Afreet!"

The girl gave a low moan and fainted. The Afreet chuckled, and lifting her in one hand. "A weak-stomached one. Well, you shall be strong enough to tell Rihman who put ideas of friends and freedom in your head! Let us see if you can be of some further use to Her Majesty before you die." Black bat wings fanned out behind the monster as he carried the unconscious girl into the depths of the tomb.

Meanwhile, Elcoloq traversed the corridors, thinking of what the captive had said. Clearly they must all escape, and soon. "This Queen Nahrit," he muttered to himself, "is not one to help me out of my enchantments. Let me stay enchanted, then! By the buried bones of forgotten ancestors, I am actually glad about that! I rather fancy my powers, and I'd hate to lose any one of them."

He felt a sudden urge to take his human shape, if only to keep in practice. Transformed, he strode through the halls until he reached the courtyard once more. His reflection in the golden basin of the fountain surprised him.

"I am no longer a boy," he mused. A tall, handsome young man stared back at him from the water. "Why is this? Well, I am human, in any case. And I am no puppy. Why should I remain a human pup as well? I do like this form."

Elcoloq leaned farther over the edge of the basin to get a better look at his new face. Human balance was a hard thing to adjust to. With a little yelp of astonishment, he toppled headfirst into the water.

"What was that?" cried the mellifluous voice of a peri

from the colonnade around the courtyard. "What was that noise?"

"I heard it! It was a splash," said a second. Elcoloq recognized the dulcet voice of Nightingale. "I am sure it was that horrible animal. A dog, isn't it?"

"Her Majesty said nothing about the dog when last I spoke with her," said the first. The fading sunlight struck the crimson gown of Pomegranate. "She said to treat the man as an honored ambassador, but do you think she would mind if we got rid of the dog?"

"Ought we?"

"You heard about what he did in the courtyard before. And now he has profaned the fountain. Do you want to spend eternity mopping up after him?"

"He won't be missed. Why not lock him up in a vacant room?"

You always were too kind, Pomegranate," said Nightingale. "Why not kill him and be done with it?"

"Yes, let's," Pomegranate agreed, approaching the fountain. The two peris drew nearer, then stopped in their tracks. "Oh! But—but—who are you?" exclaimed Pomegranate. "And where—?"

"Really, now," said the handsome youth who stood up, dripping, in the shining basin. "And would you kill the one who has been sent to save you?" The peris stared stupidly, transfixed. "I am Elcoloq," announced the youth, "Messenger of the Gods!"

Chapter XVIII

DOGMA

In a room overlaid with green and blue and white and silver tiles, hung with gauzy curtains, and furnished with cushions stuffed with rose petals, the peris lived. A little silver fountain threw a sparkling jet of scented water into the air. As it fell into the basin it made the sound of bells and flutes, lutes and harps. The peris waited there until they felt the will of Queen Nahrit summon them. There was no gossiping; one never knew when the one they slandered with some naughty tale might enter. Their sole entertainment gone, the peris were understandably bored.

But what was this? Nightingale and Pomegranate flew into the room, bearing between them a young man of very attractive features. In their day, the peris had seen many mortal men, had even beheld Lord Oran's timeless beauty, but so many years had passed since they had seen any man who interested them that they were quite captivated with this one.

"Who do you think this is?" nittered Pomegranate, all smiles.

"I am Elcoloq, Messenger of the Gods," Elcoloq repeated modestly, inclining his head a degree.

"And can you guess what he has told us?" the smug Nightingale asked in a tone that implied they would never guess at all. The other peris, in a frenzy of curiosity, rose about Elcoloq like a bonfire of butterflies, surrounding him with a fluttering brightness and all talking at once.

With a magnificent gesture he calmed them. The peris gathered at his feet in attentive silence. "The home of the gods," he began, "lies whither no man knows, yet they can see all things. Long have they watched you here, working out the time of your allotted punishment. They are moved by your plight, Daughters of Air. While they cannot end it outright, still they have sent me to offer you the chance to shorten your term of slavery."

"How?" The question sprang from a dozen pretty pairs of lips at once. Again Elcoloq motioned for them to be still.

"A simple thing will do it," he said. "A mere formality, a gesture of goodwill. The gods see that slavery is hateful to you. The gods themselves despise it. Show them, therefore, that you are willing to end the slavery of a mortal being and they will make your span of servitude shorter."

"Us? A mortal being? How can we?" asked Wisdom.

"The gods know all," Elcoloq answered severely. "Do not deny that there is at least one mortal in this tomb who wishes to be free. Do not lie to the Messenger!"

"Oh, well, the girl," said Wildrose. "Is that who the gods mean?" Elcoloq nodded. "But how can we help her?"

"The gods speak clearly," intoned the transformed dog. "Release her from bondage. You have the power to do so!"

"The power? But we do not have any power!" protested Ecstasy. "We are bound to the will of the queen. If we free the girl, we ourselves shall perish. She commands spirits that are more powerful than we, creatures of the dark beginnings of the earth. She will call them up to destroy us! Do the gods want us to die?"

"Lovely ones, be comforted. The gods will protect you," said Elcoloq. "Free the girl and trust in them."

"But it is no longer—" The speaker was Bliss. She hesitated and shivered, afraid to go on. A cold current ran through the ranks of the peris. All knew what Bliss was thinking of, and all dreaded to tell it to the Messenger.

"What?" barked Elcoloq.

"It is no longer in our hands!" Bliss blurted. "Rihman has the girl!"

The other peris moaned agreement.

"Rihman? Who is—? Oh, of course," Elcoloq amended hastily, remembering that he was supposed to be all-knowing. "Well, Rihman isn't such a big problem, is he?"

"He is an Afreet!" shrieked Harmony. "With one hand he can crush us! Oh, let the gods ask any other task of us, but do not ask us to face *him!* Will you?"

The hairs at the nape of Elcoloq's neck rose up at the name of the Afreet. Songs and tales recounted the malevolent strength of those sinister beings. The peris served Queen Nahrit under protest, but the Afreet would gladly serve any master or mistress who gave himself or herself wholeheartedly to evil.

By a mighty effort Elcoloq fought back a sick feeling of despair and forced himself to think of some way to aid the girl.

"If you fear this paltry Afreet so much," he said casually, "I can give you no hope for an end to your own bondage. But if you aid me, perhaps I can intercede with the gods for you when I return. Tell me, if the girl were not held by this Rihman, how would you save her?"

"We would not dare to do it ourselves," confessed Pearl. "Queen Nahrit sees and punishes. But we would make it possible for her to save herself. Wouldn't we?"

"Ah, a good deed!" exulted Elcoloq. "A good deed takes wing from your lips and reaches the thrones of the gods! If each one of you will add some word to what your sister has said, I swear that every hint of help you give shall cut two years from your slavery."

"All we must do is speak?" asked Wisdom.

"Good deeds are sometimes merely good words," said Elcoloq. "The girl shall be freed from the Afreet's grasp and told to flee. If your advice is good, I will pass it on to her. If she escapes the walls of this tomb, all of you shall be rewarded. The gods have spoken."

"You will conquer Rihman?" demanded Hyacinth. "Then let the girl find her own way out of the tomb. She knows the corridors well. Doesn't she?"

"But she cannot go out by the front door," protested Pomegranate. "There is another door, a hidden way of escape. It lies beneath the ground, in a catacomb of the tomb. Am I right in saying that it is concealed behind the phoenix tapestry?"

The other peris nodded. Elcoloq made an ostentatious show of tallying up the verbal good deeds of the peris, which made the remaining ones join in with their suggestions. One mentioned the best time to try an escape; one spoke of the best direction for mortals to take toward Vair; one promised to leave water bottles and traveling packs beside the phoenix tapestry. All the peris swore to be elsewhere in the tomb when the escape was tried.

"We must obey the queen," said Bliss. "But if we are all busy elsewhere, obeying a previous command, can she blame us if we do not catch the mortal girl?"

"Excellent! Excellent!" said Elcoloq, pretending to re-check the sum of good deeds on the peris' account. "Have you all spoken? Remember, each good deed subtracts two years, but each one of you who does not speak adds five years to the sum of your captivity."

There was a flutter of wings as the peris bustled about the room, obviously in high excitement. Then the uproar settled down and they thrust forward a pair of peris who might have been twins, save that one wore a most unperilike expression of sullenness and the other a look of abject fear. Elcoloq awaited an explanation.

"These are Prudence and Patience," said Nightingale, giving each a vicious pinch as she named them. Patience, the fearful one, whimpered. Prudence said nothing. "They are not really our sisters, only half-sisters. I don't like them, but I shall not spend an additional ten years in the thrall of some mortal just because they won't speak! Speak, won't you?" It was command more than question.

Prudence remained obstinate. The other peris began to rain a series of sharp cuffs and slaps upon the two silent ones until Patience covered her face and wept.

"Stop it at once!" ordered Elcoloq. "Do not strike them! We will learn nothing this way." He shoved aside the peris and gently raised Patience's face to his. "Do not cry," he said. "We only want to help you. Do you love being Queen Nahrit's slave so much? Taste freedom, fairest one. It is very sweet, I promise you. No tears! No tears! If they strike you again, the gods will destroy them."

"Indeed I am sorry that I have not spoken until now," said Patience. "My sister said it would be better not to speak. She told me that when Queen Nahrit learns of the girl's escape, she would not punish us as harshly as the others who helped you. I listened to my sister because I did not know what else to do. Do you understand?"

"But, my dear child," said Elcoloq gently, "are you so

certain that she will find out? Keep quiet and out of sight when the girl escapes, then deny you knew anything about it."

"But it won't succeed!" protested Patience. "It can't! No one has told you of the dangers to come. Others have escaped the tomb. That is easy. You can see their effigies standing frozen at the portals. Many escape the tomb, but no one escapes the Hunters of the Queen, who follow and track Queen Nahrit's slaves, and slay them in the desert. Their bones lie where none may find them. Such is the work of the Hunters of the Queen. Can't you see that it is hopeless?"

"Who are these Hunters?" demanded Elcoloq.

"They are—" Patience began. Her sister's hand snaked out and sealed her lips.

"Tell no more!" said Prudence. "Messenger of the Gods!" she sneered at Elcoloq. "Well, give them this message for us! We serve Queen Nahrit and shall serve her well, my sister and I. I would rather help her slay her enemies with the utmost cruelty than have her turn that cruelty on me. My sister is a weak and gentle thing, but I will guide her on the proper path. Let the gods send us proof of their goodwill before we help anyone else! Until I see proof, I would sooner believe in the ill will of our mistress, Queen Nahrit. I fear her more than I fear the gods, and I obey her to the death!"

Those last defiant words had scarcely left her lips when, as one being, the other peris rose up and enveloped Prudence in a cloud of brilliance, brighter than the dawning desert sun. Their voices also rose, no longer sweet; their wings beat with the thunder; their small hands darted in and out of the flaming cloud, now white as milk, now spattered red as roses. And then the pulsing, living cloud fell softly away, as the petals of an autumn flower fall, and the rebellious Prudence was no longer to be seen. Not a single peri looked at all troubled by the casual slaughter of her half-sister. A few went to rinse their bloodstained hands in the silver fountain. Only Patience wept a little.

"She will tell the queen nothing now," said Laughter. "Does that count as a good deed?"

"That . . . that remains for the gods to decide," stammered Elcoloq.

"Let us kill the other one as well," suggested Harmony.

"She will betray the girl just as her sister would have done—won't she?"

The rest of the peris set up a blithe chatter of agreement and began to crowd around the trembling Patience.

"Stop!" cried Elcoloq, thrusting himself into the midst of the splendid throng. He embraced Patience, shielding her from the deadly ones. "Leave her!" he commanded. "If the gods are displeased by this first death, they shall hate you for a second one! They shall turn their faces from you and condemn you to perpetual captivity! Let her live, I say!"

"If her life is so precious," sniffed Wisdom, "take her with you. She is a sorry excuse for a peri. Her father was a mortal. Will you still defend this half-blood?"

"Mortal lives are also precious," said Elcoloq. "She shall come with me to the home of the gods for judgment."

"Good, so long as we never see her again," said Nightingale. "We shall tell the queen that she and her sister ran away. What can you expect of such mongrels?"

"Mongrels, as you say," Elcoloq said suavely, "are highly unpredictable. Come, you!" he snapped at Patience. "The gods await my good reports of you." He left the peris laughing like schoolchildren as they wiped away Prudence's blood from the gleaming floor tiles. Patience followed him, her bright wings trailing low.

They walked through the corridors of the tomb without exchanging a word until Elcoloq came once again to the room where he had found the girl crying. A quick look and a quick sniff reassured him that no beings, visible or not, shared the room with him and Patience.

"We are safe here," he said. "Now speak on, poor little peri. You said something of the Hunters of the Queen. Who are they? How can we fight them?"

Patience gazed at the comely face of Elcoloq and sighed. "I can say no more. I have only heard of them. Warn the girl. I know of nothing you can do against them, but perhaps the gods will let you conquer them by your hidden powers."

"And what sort of powers do you mean?" asked Elcoloq.

"Why, as the Messenger of the Gods, surely you must have some special magic," said Patience earnestly. "No, you are more than their Messenger. You are a god yourself, I know it! You are too handsome to be mortal and too kind

to be a spirit of evil." The half-peri prostrated herself at
Elcoloq's feet and said, "I am your slave."

"Up!" barked Elcoloq. "Do not use that word to me! I
am not taking you to the home of the gods. That was a ruse
to save you from those vicious half-sisters of yours. If you
are a mongrel, half mortal and half peri, I'd say the breed
of peris is the better for it. You are free."

Patience raised herself on her graceful forearms and turned
wide, tear-filled eyes to Elcoloq. They were alien eyes,
holding gleaming reflections of stars and flowers, but they
were big with misery. "You do not take me? You will let
me go?" she sobbed. "Then let me return to the peris and
have them kill me! At least their cruelty and hate can end
in my death!"

"What? What's wrong? Don't you want to be free?"
asked the puzzled Elcoloq. "I thought—"

"You think I am unworthy!" shouted Patience. "You scorn
me for my mixed blood, like they did! My mother was
Grace, most beautiful of the peris, but my father was Naami
the Trickster. He deceived my mother so that she never
suspected he was mortal. When the others found out, they
slew her. I am half mortal and I will die someday, yet my
magic is as great as any of my proud full-peri sisters! Will
you believe me?"

Elcoloq was startled at this outburst from the formerly
timid Patience. "But your freedom—" he began. In answer
she grasped him by the ankles and clung to him.

"O my master, do not abandon me!" she cried. "Let me
prove my worth! Let me help the girl even as you helped
me."

So intense was Patience's plea that Elcoloq knelt beside
her on the floor and framed her ivory face with his hands.
"Sweetest of the daughters of peris and mortals," he said,
"I am Elcoloq. I am no Messenger of the Gods. I have no
special powers. I cannot take you to the home of the gods.
I do not even know where it lies. I see your heart in your
lovely eyes, dear one, and I beg of you, hold it back yet a
while. I scent love about you, but I cannot let you love me.
I cannot let you risk your life for me. Go from this tomb,
sweet Patience, and find the life that the gods intended for
you. If I were a man—"

"A dog," said Patience abruptly. "I know that. You are

the small white dog that my sisters brought here with its master. Do you think I could not see? Mortal blood gives a peri sharper eyes. I love you, Elcoloq. Dog or man, Messenger of the Gods or trickster, I love you. Whether you love me or scorn me, I will follow you and I will serve you. The beauty of your soul reaches beyond the falseness of your shape and shines with a pure and loving light."

"You love me? Even though you know I am a dog, you love me?" exclaimed Elcoloq, taking Patience in his arms and brushing her gaudy wings with his fingertips. "Can it be, or am I dreaming?"

"We are all dreaming," said Patience. "Mongrels together, you and I, we dream. Let this be a token that we never wish to wake." She kissed him.

Reluctantly Elcoloq drew his lips away from hers. "We must flee," he said. "We must find my master and the girl, then make our escape by the hidden door. Do you think we can be ready to leave this place tomorrow?"

"O my love, tomorrow is too late!" said Patience. "My sister was not the only one still faithful to Queen Nahrit. You know little of peris to trust their words. Many of them will run to tell the queen of this proposed escape as soon as they can. They think to keep the goodwill of both the queen and the gods."

"They are treacherous for all their beauty," said Elcoloq grimly. "But they risk much in seeking to deceive the gods. Your sister was the only honest one."

"Honesty in this place earns death. So does delay. The queen is contemplating killing. She has gone into her retreat. Each time she does, a mortal dies. Follow me."

Patience seized Elcoloq's hand and led him from the vacant chamber through the twisting corridors. She stopped at a shadowed archway. "It is almost sunset," she said. "Our time runs short. I will show you why, but then we must move quickly, quickly. Come!"

Within the archway was a curtain. This she lifted to reveal a small wooden door, which opened at a gently spoken word. Beyond it lay blackness. "Come," repeated Patience, and she guided Elcoloq into the unseen that lay beyond the portal. As he followed, she spoke a second word and the door drifted shut behind them. They were alone in the secret dark.

Chapter XIX

MAD DOG

Elcoloq's eyes grew used to the dark slowly. He mused that there were advantages to being born a cat after all. Silently he moved, even his breathing hushed. The hard, cold grip of Patience's small fingers on his arm told him wordlessly that sound would mean discovery—and discovery would mean death.

Shapes filtered through the dark. A short distance ahead of him he saw the outline of a railing, arabesques of iron against the shadows. Tiles were beneath his feet. As Patience led him on, he saw that the railing belonged to a balcony that wound off and lost itself in night. Patience released his arm so that he might grasp the railing. With both hands firm around the iron bar, he ventured to look down.

He expected to see only darkness, with perhaps the moonlit glimmer of another tile floor below. Instead he peered into a maze of curling, twisting, tangling clouds of smoke, a sight out of the heart of a burning mountain. Like silver serpents they wound about each other, tracing luminous spirals and sinuous designs. They danced to unheard music and then, at some touch of an invisible hand, were torn asunder like misty curtains to reveal a wondrous scene.

Upon a floor of shining bronze, traced all over with scarlet signs and symbols, stood a massy platform made of malachite. It was impossible to see all of it from the balcony. A curtain of black velvet shot with crimson threads hid part of it from sight. Before this curtain smoked a brazen dish, heaped high with fragrant gums and spices. If anything lurked behind the curtain, they could not see it.

A woman lay prostrate on the floor, her face pressed hard against it. Her outstretched arms lay extended toward the altar; her hair fell free upon her shoulders. A crown lay beside her, a crown set round with winking tiger's-eye, and a golden wand lay just beyond her grasp. Elcoloq recalled seeing the crown and wand before, worn by the sham queen Nahrit. Something struck him about the woman who was flat upon the floor of brass: A feeling of terrible strength surrounded her. Here lay no sham queen, no puppet, but she who made the puppets dance and she who called the tunes.

But she looks so old! he exclaimed to himself with wonder. Her hair is streaked with white and silver, and now she lifts up her face—old! Dry as leather it appears, withered as last year's autumn. The wrinkles lace her cheeks; her eyes are deep-set, burning with unnatural force. She strains the limits of her body; her very bones press too sharply against that aged and fragile skin. She will devour herself with her own flame!

The old woman got painfully to her feet and stretched out her hands above the brazier, gray whorls of smoke twining gently amid the ashen strands of her trailing hair.

"Master!" she cried out to the darkness. "Thy servant awaits thy presence. Do not leave your faithful one to call to thee in vain, but answer me. Answer me!"

There was silence in the chamber as the smoke wove upward in the gloom. Then a voice—drier than the many deaths of wasted summers, darker than the caverns of the moon—came gliding coldly as a viper from behind the ebon curtain. "Speak," it said. "I attend you."

"O master! Thy fondest hopes have been accomplished! My seclusion in this tomb has not been in vain. Not for nothing have I feigned death before the world; not for nothing have my years been wasted in the confines of the desert. Master, I bring thee now thy greatest triumph!"

A ghastly exultation illuminated the withered features of the suppliant. Waiting stillness answered her. "A messenger has come to me. He bears an offer—an offer—" In her joy she could hardly go on. "—an offer of marriage from—O heed me, master!—from Ayree!"

"Ayree?" the voice behind the curtain hissed. "You are sure? Ayree, the Prince of Warlocks, whose sisters may—?"

"The same, the very same!" She laughed madly, joyously, head thrown back and toothless mouth agape. "We shall not have to worry about Ayree's precious sisters for long, my lord!"

"That is good. They have eluded me and my creatures. With each day that passes they grow older, and if I cannot prevent it, they will destroy me!"

"They shall not," said the woman. "I have accomplished by waiting what all of your servants in the north could not do. We shall bring them out of the north and deal with them. And then shall the Older Empire flourish anew, and the world shall be thine to do with what thou wilt. None shall dare to rise against thee again, nor trouble me. The world itself shall be—" The woman clenched her hands in greed and hunger.

"Shall be . . . whose?" There was a gentle menace in the voice, as if it could be amused to a point, but would not hesitate to punish arrogance to the fullest degree. The woman caught the hint and bowed her head.

"It shall be thine," came the chastened reply. "All I ask is my throne and my youth. Each time that you renew me, it does not last as long. Each time I grow older and more hideous. Master, have I offended you?"

"Questions sound better on other lips," said the voice coldly. "My servants ask none. Step forward. It is the time of your renewal. I would not have you forget that it is I alone who grant you your beauty again. You are a daughter of pride, Nahrit. I will break you of it. But now, where is the promised sacrifice?"

"My lord, it shall be given to thee with the dawn. The girl is beautiful and gentle. You will find her fitting. This one time I beseech thee to grant my renewal before the sacrifice is made. I must return to Ayree's messenger and press him to arrange the wedding day soon. He must not see me like this."

"I do not grant my gifts without payment. You know what shall become of you if you do not make the sacrifice at the promised hour?"

"Do with me as thou wilt, but renew me now!" flared

Nahrit. "I am the queen among thy servants, and I swear by the heart of Oran that you will be satisfied with my offering! Behold! She is surely yours, my lord, and in the most secure of keeping!" Queen Nahrit threw out her arms and in a flash of reeking, oily smoke, Rihman the Afreet appeared, clutching the fragile body of the girl in one upraised hand.

"If she is here, why delay the sacrifice?" asked the voice. The Afreet heard it and recognized the speaker. Clumsily he knelt beside the queen, head low and palms outstretched in submission. The girl was set down on the metal floor.

"My minion tells me that she has knowledge of something that may endanger us. I fear that other powers have entered my tomb and seek to destroy me. If they succeed before I can weave my spells around Ayree, then we are doomed."

"'We'?" mocked the voice. "Not we, my queen. But I would be sorry to lose so faithful a servant as yourself. Question the girl, but make her mine by the dawning. Do not deceive me. Morgeld's arm is long to claim that which belongs to him!"

"I shall remember it, my lord. And Nahrit belongs—in soul, in heart, in body—most happily to Morgeld!"

The smoke from the brazier now began to glow with golden lights, to glitter as if the eyes of a thousand serpents were peering out of it, twining their long bodies around Queen Nahrit's arms, lovingly embracing her sagging, ancient neck, stealing over all her body until she was gone from sight, wrapped in a hazy cloud of flickering, trembling, dancing lights.

The cloud dispersed. Queen Nahrit—the young, the beautiful, the tawny-haired, the one who wore starlight—stood tall and proud upon the sanctuary floor. The transformation was complete. She laughed.

"By dawn thou shalt have her, my lord! Never doubt that Nahrit keeps her promises."

"That is good," said the voice, fading away in the drifting smoke, "for Morgeld always fulfills his."

The brazier glowed on, but the smoke was gone. Queen Nahrit placed the crown on her head and gathered up her golden wand before confronting the Afreet. The girl had crawled as far away from that evil pair as she could, but

she could not find door or window to lead her out of the
brazen room. She huddled herself in a corner and waited.

"Learn what you can from her, Rihman," commanded
the queen. "Make her talk by any means you like. But leave
no mark on her. She must go to Morgeld at dawn. If she
does not speak by then, we must take a chance that any
alien powers will be too weak to fight me here or to prevent
my marriage to Ayree." Without another word, Nahrit vanished.

Elcoloq felt a tug at his elbow. Patience and he retraced
their steps back through the little door into the corridor and
let the curtain down over it.

"Now do you see?" she whispered, glancing furtively
about as she spoke. "It must be tonight! At dawn the girl
will die!"

"You are right," he agreed. "This Queen Nahrit has done
more than merely while away the ages within her tomb. I
do not know the full length of all she has done or the meaning
of all that she said in that haunted chamber. I think I am
happier not knowing. We leave tonight. I shall rescue the
girl and bring her to Mustapha; then we flee."

"Beloved of my heart," said Patience, twining her arms
around Elcoloq's neck and placing a gentle kiss on his lips.
"You have no weapons. How shall you save her from Rihman? He would destroy you, and that would destroy me.
You cannot hope to do it alone. Let us venture together."

"Never! I will not let you face the Afreet, my sweet
one!" objected Elcoloq. "Even if I am unarmed, I will find
a rescue by cunning. Man or dog, I am sharp-witted enough
to convince that monster that he is a newborn lamb and to
make him run bleating off in search of his mother."

"I do not like this," said Patience. "Together we
could—"

"If I am not at Mustapha's door within the hour, tell him
to leave without me. Show him the way from this tomb and
the road to Vair. He was always good to me," said Elcoloq.
He turned from Patience and slipped back into the room of
brass.

Torches, mysteriously suspended in the air above the
altar, cast wavering shadows upon the Afreet and the girl.
Her long hair had been transformed into a leash, which the

monster wrapped once around her neck and tugged at roughly for his own amusement.

"You heard the queen!" the Afreet's voice boomed and echoed in the brazen room. "Whether or not you speak, you die! But speak, and spare yourself much pain before your death. Queen Nahrit said there must be no marks on you. Do you think that will limit me? I am old, little bird. I know arcane ways to inflict untold suffering, never leaving a mark any bigger than the touch of a falling leaf. Speak, fool, and spare yourself."

The girl sobbed dryly and could not answer. Her eyes remained fixed on the squashed and ugly face of the Afreet. Rihman gnashed his tusks impatiently and yanked sharply at the rope of tawny hair.

"I am not asking you for a spell to wake the Hidden Sleeper, girl! I ask a simple thing! What friend did you babble of? Is it a mortal or a spirit? Is it a shape of good or evil for us? Is it still here? Tell me, and have the satisfaction of seeing me slay it before we slay you tomorrow!"

"I—I know nothing," gasped the girl. "But if I did know, I would take my knowledge to my grave! I pray that he was a spirit of good who came to me. May he return and send you back to the caves of eternal darkness, Rihman! May your collar be broken and your voice be stilled forever!"

The light of wicked mirth in the Afreet's eyes perished at her words. One hand still on the rope of hair, Rihman reached up to touch the narrow blue enamel band that ringed his neck. It might easily have girdled a young oak tree. "Do you dare?" he roared. "Do you dare to offer that curse to me? You shall be forgotten dust before my collar lies in pieces! The man does not live who shall conquer it or me!"

"It shall be broken. It shall!" the girl shouted back, defiant through her terror. "I have read much, Rihman! I know the prophecy of your name and of your fate. I may die, but your death awaits you just as certainly."

The Afreet seized the girl as a child might seize a rag doll. He raised her level with his gaping mouth and roared his rage in her face. "Let your readings and your prophecies end here! I will enjoy killing you, ill-omened one!"

"Tut, tut, Rihman!" came the high, sharp voice of Elcoloq. "Queen Nahrit will not be pleased to find that her servant has deprived Morgeld of his sacrifice."

The Afreet wheeled and searched the chamber, but saw no one. He ground his yellow teeth together in perplexity.

"Up here, fool!" prompted the voice. Rihman swiftly looked up and saw a small white form perched high above him on the iron balcony. The vision wagged its tail and barked with delight at the monster's puzzlement.

"Who are you?" shouted Rihman. In answer, Elcoloq sat back on his haunches and scratched behind one ear.

"I? I am the answer to the questions you were asking that poor girl. I am the friend she spoke of and the spirit you fear. I am Elcoloq, Beloved of Ayree!"

"Ayree! I do not fear that name!" The Afreet laughed, setting down the girl and turning his full attention to the dog on the balcony. "He commands the sorceries of a child! Never did I understand why my mistress feared him so much."

"That may be because your mistress has a brain where you have only an empty crock of clay!" replied Elcoloq. "Look at me, Rihman! See what Ayree has made me and tremble!"

"He has made a dog talk. What is there to fear in that?" scoffed the Afreet, but he touched his collar to ward off bad luck, just to be safe.

"In that, nothing. But I could always talk. You can talk, too, and you are more of a pig than a dog. Yes, I talked— talked too much and talked once too often—for I was once Elcoloq, Lord of Djin, and see to what a state Ayree has reduced me."

The Afreet was skeptical. "You, a Djin? I ride the winds with the Djin, and never once did I hear them speak of you."

"Who remembers a fallen king?" said Elcoloq philosophically. "I ruled the earth in the days when the Older Empire was a clutch of goatskin tents on the desert and you were still a nightmare. I commanded hordes of Djin, and under our eyes we saw the Older Empire grow. It amused us to allow these mortal creatures to flourish for a while before we destroyed them. This time the kill was to be mine. I rode the thundercloud down over the city, but before I could unleash my magic, I saw a second cloud come streaming toward me out of the north. On it rode the young Prince of Warlocks, he they call Ayree. My stupid brother, have you ever seen a duel of magic?"

"Aye," replied the Afreet slowly. "My own magics are few, but I have witnessed such duels. The Djin hold more powers of enchantment than the peris or the Afreets. Did you not conquer the warlock?"

"Does it look as if I did?" snarled Elcoloq. "Here, give me your hand and set me down on the floor. I have important things to tell you." Obediently the Afreet made a carpet of his hand and wafted Elcoloq gently down from the iron balcony. "Good," said Elcoloq once his feet touched the floor. "Now hark, Rihman. If Ayree could turn a Djin into a dog to do his bidding, what do you think he will do to an Afreet?"

"He will do nothing! He weds my mistress soon and he will not harm her servants!"

"Perhaps not, but— Bend down, Rihman. I must whisper this in your ear." The Afreet knelt beside the dog and turned one hairy ear toward him. Elcoloq's keen eyes darted around the edge of the blue collar, seeking the fastening that held it on. He groaned inwardly when he saw that it was cast of a single continuous strip of metal.

"Well, go on," said the Afreet. "What must you tell me?"

"I must tell you that if you wish to save yourself on the day that Ayree becomes your king, you must not have the blood of this mortal girl on your hands," decreed Elcoloq. The Afreet started, but Elcoloq went boldly on. "Look at her, Rihman! Have you not heard of Ayree's sisters? I tell you, this is the fabled thirteenth sister of Ayree, stolen by demons from her icy cradle on the day of her birth and left in the desert. Think of the reward you may demand if the Prince of Warlocks finds her safe! Think of your punishment if he learns that you have killed her!"

"What would you have me do?" asked the Afreet in a suspiciously docile manner. "Lord of the Djin, what would you have me do?"

"Release her!" ordered Elcoloq. "Set the girl free at once and let me return her to her brother. Your name will have praise from my lips."

"Certainly I will free her, master," the Afreet said hastily.

"But tell me, what shall we do tomorrow for the promised sacrifice? Morgeld demands it, O Lord of the Djin. What will you say to Morgeld?"

"To Morgeld I will send a flute and tell him to go piping for the girl!" exclaimed Elcoloq in a fine burst of confidence. He leaped to his hind legs and did a little jig of delight, silently congratulating himself for having so completely baffled and deceived the fearsome Afreet. He would have laughed aloud if he dared.

The hand of Rihman swooped down and slammed the breath out of Elcoloq, sending him hurtling across the floor to collide with the wall of brass. Flashes of red and yellow exploded before his eyes, and the floor tilted horribly beneath him. He tried to stand, but dizzying blackness confused his senses and the booming laughter of Rihman reverberated painfully in his buzzing ears.

"Lord of the Djin indeed!" howled the Afreet. "What Lord of Djin would have so little brain as to scorn the true master of all darkness? Who is the stupid one now, false one? I shall bring you and your sorry stories before Queen Nahrit. Then we shall see how well you can tell fantastic tales!"

The Afreet had raised his hand for a second blow when a sweet voice distracted him. "Well done, Rihman! Her Majesty will be pleased." The peri Patience smiled down upon the loathsome Afreet from the height of the iron balcony. With a light step she perched on the railing and glided down the stairway of the air to reach Rihman's side. From mortal size she grew to equal Rihman in height, and her beauty grew accordingly. The Afreet passed one hand before his eyes to shield them from the dazzle of her wings.

"You have done well," repeated Patience. "I thank the powers that we serve for that! You and I, Rihman, were not deceived by this lying dog and all his pretty tales. We know where our allegiance lies. I have spied on him ever since he entered the tomb, and I have spied on you as well, by the queen's orders."

"What? Does Her Majesty not trust me?" complained Rihman.

"Your loyalty, but not your intelligence," said Patience. "I was the one who said to her that you would prove yourself.

'If you believe this,' she answered me, 'what will you stake on it?'"

"Her Majesty is passionately fond of gambling," admitted the Afreet. "What did you wager?"

"I wagered something that would let me win by losing," said Patience, hovering nearer to the Afreet. Her gleaming arms shone like moonlit alabaster through the tender gauze of her dress. Elcoloq watched, his heart breaking with a pain he had never imagined, as the peri wove herself around the towering body of Rihman. "I wagered my love," said Patience.

The Afreet hardly dared to move, as confused by his good fortune as any mortal would be in similar circumstances. The peri ran her fingers delicately down the trailing moustachios of the monster and breathed kisses on the deformed face. The Afreet began to gain courage and closed his arms about the fair peri. Elcoloq stumbled to his feet, his head clear, and tried to lunge at Rihman. The girl quickly took his collar in her hand and restrained him. The miserable dog strained against it impotently, then threw himself to the floor and howled.

Rihman regarded him with scorn, Patience still in his arms.

"Do you see, O Lord of the Djin? This is my reward for loyalty! We shall slay the girl at dawn, but we shall save your death to celebrate our marriage feast! This is the pay of Queen Nahrit's true servants!"

"The pay is death," said Patience quietly. She gave a short, sharp twist with the fingers of her right hand, hidden under the Afreet's tangled, greasy locks. A harsh, cold sound of snapping metal rang from the brazen walls of the secret chamber and the blue enamel collar of Rihman fell shattered at his feet.

The brazen room became a sounding bell that caught and magnified the anguish of Rihman's howls. The Afreet clutched at his throat, feeling for the collar that was no longer there, while at his feet a web of darkness began to spread, sending up choking spirals of obsidian smoke. Patience hung sparkling in midair, mortal size once more, watching grimly. A cage of night rose up and covered the Afreet like the inexorably closing fingers of a giant black hand, and then the shape of horror sank swiftly out of sight, leaving not a shadow of its passing on the brazen floor.

Patience alighted beside Elcoloq and the girl. She hugged the dog close, happy tears in her eyes. Elcoloq's own joy was so great that he forgot words and barked instead.

"Ah, my love, did you think I would betray you?" said Patience, stroking his sleek head.

"I . . . I did not know," admitted the dog.

Patience smiled. "You see now that I was right," she said. "Together we have conquered. Now we must be even quicker to escape. The queen will want to see Rihman and the girl before dawn, and other peris may already have given the alarm of our flight. Hurry!" She extended her hands to the girl and Elcoloq, who disguised himself in human form. One arm around each mortal, Patience spread her wings, flew to the balcony, and took them through the first door of many on their route to freedom.

The corridor on the other side of the door was quiet. "Let us separate," said Elcoloq. "I must fetch Mustapha from his room. We shall meet in the hall of tapestries."

"Yes, the tapestry of the phoenix," said Patience. She looked to the girl for agreement, but the poor child had undergone too much to do more than follow the first person who would lead her anywhere. "Do not be afraid," said Patience. "The time has come to stop thinking of all peris as your jailors. I am Patience, half peri and half mortal, even as you are mortal. Take my hand, child. We must be gone ere moonrise." The girl ventured a shy smile and willingly gave Patience her hand.

"Good," said Elcoloq. "If my master and I are not at the tapestry of the phoenix by the time the first star is seen, go the two of you alone. The girl is in greater danger than we are."

"It shall be as you say," Patience acquiesced. "But I am not sure who is in the greater peril. If Queen Nahrit cannot find one sacrifice, she may choose another. Fare you well!"

Patience left swiftly in a flurry of wings, drawing the girl after her. He watched the beauty of her going, then dropped to hands and knees. Soon a small white dog was trotting away down the empty hall.

Elcoloq found Mustapha's door and, in the manner of common dogs begging entrance, began to scrape his claws against it and whine. To his surprise the first touch of his paws pushed the door open. He entered slowly, mistrusting this easy access to his master.

Mustapha lay stretched motionless on one of the divans. A cold, an unspeakable cold, touched the good dog to the heart. Had they slain his master? What need to lock up a dead man? He leaped forward—barking, whining, growling all at once—and landed full on Mustapha's stomach.

Whoof!

Mustapha sat up, gasping for breath and clutching his assaulted stomach. Elcoloq jumped lightly to the ground, tongue lolling in a doggy grin. "What is the meaning of this, Elcoloq?" demanded the winded Mustapha. "Do I wake you up in such a rude fashion? I thought you would never return, and I have had a strange interview since you were gone."

"No stranger than mine, I'll wager," said the dog. Tersely he told Mustapha all that had passed. Mustapha could only shake his head in amazement.

"So that is how she has come to live so long!" he mused. "It is a miracle that the smell of death is not stronger upon her. I did well to listen to your advice, my friend. Guide me again. What shall we do now?"

"Do? Leave, of course—at once. Patience and the girl shall meet us in the hall of tapestries. If we traverse the Desert of Thulain in the company of a peri—or even a half-peri—we have a better chance of coming out alive."

"I fear this tomb more than the desert, and I greatly fear the unseen one who spoke to Queen Nahrit from behind the black curtain. We have heard his name before."

"In truth I have but a dog's memory for names. Queen Nahrit has more to fear from him than we do, if she does not bring him his sacrifice at dawn."

"We will be long gone by dawn," said Mustapha, rising from the divan. "This gaudy prison stifles me, and my heart hates this luxurious captivity more than our time among Lord Olian's people. Can you find the hall of tapestries?"

"My nose can sniff out more than game," said Elcoloq. "We are as good as there." On cautious feet they left the room and sped through the winding passageways of Queen Nahrit's tomb, their minds fixed on the phoenix tapestry and freedom.

Chapter XX

FIRE DOGS

Patience had given Elcoloq excellent directions. Now the dog easily led Mustapha through the sharp turns and seemingly endless corridors to the hall of the tapestries. After a time of twisting and backtracking, the floor appeared to turn downward, sometimes swerving gently, sometimes doubling back, but always slanting down, down to where there were no longer even window-slits, where there were no small courtyards, where the walls gave off the damp and humid exhalations of a dungeon.

They passed many doors. Some were as finely wrought as the most precious jewelry; some were merely brass-bound wood; some were hewn of stone. They could hear only their own footsteps and, from far away, the sound of water trickling.

The corridor ended in a tall and narrow door covered with soft white leather and studded with massive silver nails. The whole portal was a work of supreme artistry.

"The world has lost many things with the passing of the Older Empire," sighed Mustapha. "Think, Elcoloq! If their common doors look like this, what their palaces must have looked like!"

Elcoloq did not reply. He thought of the slaves who had to build those palaces and make those doors. He snorted and pawed at the white leather. There was no handle.

"Here's a pickle!" said Mustapha. "How are we to get in?"

"Master, I could help you if—" A young man stood beside Mustapha, grinning. Together they put their shoulders

148

to the door and pushed. It ceded before them, and they barely kept themselves from tumbling headfirst into the room beyond.

Mustapha gasped. A single torch burned dim in its socket. The feeble light, reflected upon the piles of gems, the casks of silver, the vessels of purest gold, doubled and redoubled in brilliance until it dazzled the beholder. The wealth of ages, the wealth of kings, the hoard of the monarchs of the Older Empire lay heaped at the ill-shod feet of Mustapha of Vair.

It took Elcoloq but a moment to recover from his first sight of such riches. In an instant he was on his knees, looking for a sack among the mounts of blue-white diamonds, the strands of starry pearls. Finding none, he seized instead a silver casket and filled it brimful with gems, scorning the ordinary gold and silver coins.

Mustapha did not join Elcoloq in harvesting gems. Rather, he gazed about the chamber at his leisure, lost in dreams of the past. For what price had each piece of gold been bought? What price each shining jewel? This emerald ring a man might well have died for; and that sapphire might have won a war. Here was a diadem of moonlight set with stars, for surely no silversmith could make such magic of mere earthly metals. What princess had put out her hands to place this crown upon her flowery hair? Where lay the robes that she had worn, the prince that she had wed? Gone, all gone; only the crown remained, unseen by all the world, knowing the silent story.

A peculiar object attracted Mustapha as he wandered in the treasure house. It was a thing out of place, a tube made of black wood the length of Mustapha's arm from elbow to fingertips. Round plugs of heavy silver sealed each end, and from these dangled tassels of fine silver chain. The tube also had a thick silver chain attached around its middle, making it look as if the thing had once been worn around somebody's neck. An odd necklace! thought Mustapha. He picked it up and slipped the chain over his head to see how it felt. He was about to remove it again when Elcoloq grabbed his arm and said it was time to go on.

Another door stood at the far end of the treasure house, and through this they passed. It opened into a kind of minor armory, most likely the guardroom for the vaults. There were no fancy weapons—only good, serviceable swords, spears, and crossbows of ancient design. Time—and larvae—had eaten through the wooden hafts of the spears, and the bowstrings had all fallen to dust. Mustapha scrounged up a pair of not-too-rusty swords and gave one to Elcoloq. Feeling a bit more secure, they left the guardroom by a second door and found themselves in the great hall of the tapestries.

"Elcoloq, this is better than the greatest library in all the world!" exclaimed Mustapha, looking about him with rapture.

The room had many walls. It was not designed after any simple shape of geometry, but had numerous alcoves and superfluous corners to create extra wall space. Glorious tapestries covered every wall from floor to ceiling. Sometimes one immense tapestry covered a wall, sometimes two smaller ones shared it, and sometimes a veritable patchwork of the woven treasures curtained the masonry.

"Look, master," said Elcoloq. "The torches in this room are fresh."

"Aye, and the tapestries are still brilliant. Here there is no sign of neglect, as in the armory. The queen frequents this room; but that is no wonder. With what else can she amuse herself? The peris are not good for deep conversation. Here she can walk with the heroes and villains of the legendary times and see their exploits acted out for her anew. Behold! On yonder wall a series of pictures illustrating the last hunt of the sea king, Telaris. And see there—the death of Andiri, the marriage of Ambra! And that bold warrior could only be Lord Oran himself."

"Master, if that be Oran, we see no picture book of legends. We walk through history. Remember, this queen is no young maiden. She has walked and talked with those we call the men of myth. We see Lord Oran with sword in hand, proud in battle, but for her Oran was just another dinner guest. I am sure she has passed the salt and salad to a number of heroes in her day."

Mustapha did not reply. He continued to examine the tapestries. "We can waste no more time," he said. "We must find the tapestry of the phoenix." The infinite corners, archways, vaults, and recesses of the hall made it an open maze.

Only by diligent search would they find the tapestry that hid the secret door. Elcoloq was little help.

"Master, what does a phoenix look like?"

"It is a large bird."

"Oh," said Elcoloq, and proceeded to point out peacocks, quail, pheasants, partridges, and once a roasted turkey in a banquet scene.

"That can't be it," Elcoloq mumbled, running from wall to wall. "No birds there. None there, either. Is that it?"

"That's a widgeon. Haven't you ever seen a widgeon before?" Mustapha yelled back, intent on his own search.

"'Haven't you ever seen a widgeon before?'" sneered Elcoloq. "Oh, yes! All the time, master! Why, the widgeons used to just flock around the alley I lived in. Stop by for dinner, they would! Oh, certainly!"

"What did you say?" demanded Mustapha.

"I said I thought this was the one, down this little hall, but on second thought it can't be. The bird's all on fire and half burned up."

"On fire?" Mustapha raced to Elcoloq's side and found himself staring at the biggest, most majestic royal tapestry of all, depicting the self-immolation of the fabled phoenix on a pyre of spicewood. Small winged spirits watched from the borders while to the left of the pyre maidens wept and to the right heroes threw their swords into the flames.

"Elcoloq, remind me to see to your education when I can," said Mustapha. *"That* is a phoenix." In his human form, Elcoloq enjoyed the luxury of shrugging his shoulders. Then, in the shadows cast beneath the torches, they perceived something moving. There was a soft rustling and two figures stepped out in front of the tapestry.

Both were heavily veiled and swathed in traveling robes, voluminous but light. Patience's brilliant wings made two unsightly bulges beneath her garment. A third bump disfigured the girl's back, certainly a sack of provisions for their flight. Mustapha knelt before them, taking Patience's hand with one of his own and the girl's hand with his other.

"I am Mustapha, your humble servant," he said. "I will do all that is within my power to aid you. My strength, my heart, my life, my sword I pledge to you."

The girl thanked him silently with her eyes. Patience had

no time for fine words and tender looks. "Come, we must be away!" she declared, lifting the right-hand corner of the tapestry. A low door stood behind it, already open and breathing out the damp reek of long-abandoned passageways. Into this dank and evil-smelling place the peri vanished and they followed.

The way behind the tapestry was a smaller version of the mazy tomb, only so full of foulness, brooding melancholy, menacing darkness, and icy winds, that the traveler was tempted to hold his nose with one hand, his companion's hand with the other, and wish for a third hand to clutch his robes closer about him.

"What is this place?" whispered the girl, stumbling through the shadows and shuddering each time her hands brushed the clammy walls.

"In the days before Lord Oran's death," said Patience, "Queen Nahrit thought to build her tomb as a tomb, not as the retreat it became. The entrance through which you first came was added later. This passage was to be the only way in or out; no visible entrance would exist to tempt graverobbers who'd heard tales of treasure. A great architect designed it, and many slaves labored to build it. But when Queen Nahrit changed her plans, the passage was forgotten."

"Forgotten," said the echo. "Forgotten . . . forgotten . . . forgotten. . . ." A blast of cold air pierced their clothes and made them gasp for breath.

"Where do these winds come from?" asked Mustapha, fingers closing around the hilt of his newly acquired sword. "Are we near the end of the maze?"

"Not yet," said Patience.

Something with wings zagged above their heads, then chittered when it dove and got tangled in a fold of the girl's robes. Elcoloq reached down to release it, and it whirred away into the darkness.

"We need a torch," said Elcoloq. "This false cavern has spawned eyeless beasts. It would be better if we saw them before they saw us."

"Hush," Patience replied. "There are no branching routes in this passage. We have no need of a light. It might attract things that are better left undisturbed."

"But I don't like this!" protested Elcoloq. "I've fallen twice and grazed my shins more times than I like. Are you afraid of moths? Strike a light, I say!"

"Hush, Elcoloq," cautioned Mustapha. "The peri has dwelt here longer than we. She has her reasons."

"What are they, then?" demanded Elcoloq, out of temper. As he spoke, his foot caught on something in his path and he fell heavily forward to the rough stone floor. The other three gathered around to help him to his feet. "Enough!" cried Elcoloq, shaking them off. "Let me at least see what it was that nearly made me break my neck!" He seized the hem of Patience's cape and tore it free. The peri's wings shed a bright golden light over the narrow passageway.

The girl looked down and screamed, for what Elcoloq had stumbled over was a skeleton, most of the bones scattered and gone but the skull and ribs still plain to see. A thin bronze axe lay among the yellowing bones.

"The secret of Queen Nahrit's tomb was to remain safe until the end of time," Patience said sadly. "The slaves were all killed. Then the queen decided to change the tomb's design and keep it like a palace of death. The slaves had died for nothing. They say the architect was also put to death, so that the secret of the tomb would never be disclosed.

"Sprinkle a handful of dust over the bones and leave them. We must go on."

The soft light cast by the peri's wings did little to cheer the weeping stones of the passage. The warmth of that glow was greedily drunk in by the sallow walls and reflected from the drab patches of moss that clung there with a sickly greenish tinge.

Mustapha held his hand out and said, "I liked this better in the dark. I look as if the Braegerd fever had claimed me."

"The way grows narrower," said Patience, pausing to address the others. "We must keep stricter single file. At least my light will be of some help here. There are small recesses in the wall from this point on. They must have been the sentry boxes of the poor wretches who would have been buried alive to guard Queen Nahrit's remains. Do not enter them. I have heard rumors that the tomb's architect designed some of them as plain alcoves, but caused deep pits to be dug in others, to lure tomb robbers to their deaths. Follow me with care."

"I'll follow Patience," said Elcoloq. "Master, you follow me, and the girl should bring up the rear. We have no fear of pursuit, but she carries that sack on her shoulders; were she to strike either of us with it by accident, it might knock us into one of those delightful pits that Patience speaks of. Do you mind coming last?" he asked the girl.

"Not now, when we have light to see by," she said. The travelers fell into line, and Patience conducted them on through the narrowing halls.

As the peri had said, they passed the alcoves and saw pits excavated in some of them. Patience quickened the pace, eager to be out in the desert's fresh air. Her wings felt cold, and their glow faded with a nameless dread that crept up on her as she threaded the corridors. She fanned her wings to shake it off but could not. The light dimmed from gold to pale yellow, then to the ashy gray of winter twilight.

At the end of the procession, the girl found herself hard pressed to keep up with this sudden haste, unused as she was to exertion after her years of palace life. She had to stop and rest. Without a word to Mustapha, she leaned gasping against the wall of the maze and watched the others move ahead.

The light of Patience's wings was not entirely gone by the time the girl was ready to go on. Exercising great care to avoid the alcoves, she sprinted after her companions. The glow grew stronger as she drew nearer and seemed to have taken on an emerald tinge. She could not suppress a happy cry as she rounded a bend in the corridor and laid one hand on the caped back of Mustapha. The shining light before him was almost blinding in brilliance.

He turned at her touch, and the girl saw the source of the green light: Two living fires the color of emeralds burned hideously bright in the eyeless sockets of a fleshless skull. Its bony jaws dropped open and a mirthless laugh echoed and reechoed in the close space of the tomb.

The girl screamed and tried to run, but her hands were seized in naked claws. She struggled uselessly as the creature drew out a length of rusty chain from its tattered cloak and clapped strange white manacles on her wrists.

Mustapha heard the scream some distance behind him, and the hollow laughter. He turned swiftly. "She is gone!" he cried, shaking Elcoloq by the shoulder.

"Where could she go?" demanded Elcoloq. The last notes of the creature's merriment reached his ears and made the hair on the back of his neck stand on end. "Patience!" he cried. The peri turned. "The girl is gone!"

Without a word, Patience slid past Mustapha and El-coloq, then raced down the corridor to follow the dying sound of the girl's cries. Her wings blazed up gloriously again, and fear for the little mortal almost made her fly. Elcoloq and Mustapha pounded after her.

"Stop! You have gone back too far!" called Elcoloq. His voice sounded sad and lone in the passageway. "Look there." He pointed to the packed earth floor. The signs of a struggle were plain to see. He stooped down and picked up something small, hard, and white. "A bone," he said. "The joint of a finger or toe, perhaps. I mislike this." He threw himself flat to examine the trail as best he could in human form. Faint scuff marks led into one of the alcoves. "Over there," he said finally.

Patience spread her wings for better light. The alcove in question had a floor, and on this floor were traces of something being dragged. The marks ended at the stone walls.

"It must be a door," said Patience. "Be very careful, for what thing can dwell in this lost part of the tomb, and what can it want with the mortal girl?" She placed her right hand on the curved rear wall of the alcove and chanted a queerly accented melody, a spell of opening. The stones groaned like rusty hinges and slid back into darkness.

"We have him!" shouted Elcoloq, brandishing his sword and leaping past Patience into the gap. "We have—"

Mustapha's heart lurched as Elcoloq's voice abruptly rose into a cry of surprise and then dissolved into a howl of terror. He would have plunged into the yawning hole in the wall after his friend, but Patience held him back.

"You and he shall meet the same fate if you do not show some judgment," she said earnestly. "Let me go first to light the way." Mustapha nodded and reluctantly put up his sword.

The peri stepped daintily through the gap, her wings bright. Mustapha heard a little gasp of comprehension and a laugh of relief. He went after her and saw what had happened to his loyal dog.

Elcoloq had fallen into a simple kind of trap: a pit. In earlier days the hole might have been deeper, but drifting dust had reduced its depth to scarcely seven feet. The transformed dog had had a soft though undignified landing. Mustapha gave him a hand in clambering out.

"Where are we now?" Elcoloq wondered. They tried to pierce the darkness with the light from the peri's wings. A pale green light shone from many walls, the crazy tag ends of a series of passageways. They flitted from one to another of the darkened archways, seeing only long halls that led to nowhere.

"I must take the scent better," said Elcoloq. The young man vanished, his sword clattering to the floor. Even as Mustapha bent to pick up the weapon, the small white dog put his nose to the ground and cast about for the spoor. Back and forth he zigzagged until at last he yapped success and dashed away.

The others followed him up a short corridor, made to seem longer by madly angled corners and impossible twists. Then they spilled into a round room where the greenish light was so strong that it dripped from the walls and lay in stagnant pools of phosphorescence. The sound of the girl's cries struck them as soon as they entered.

She was fettered to the curving wall with chain gone russet with corrosion and smooth manacles of a disturbingly milky appearance. A raggedly clothed figure hunched like a poisonous toad at her feet. It turned to face their intrusion, letting them see its gruesome countenance. Even the peri could not suppress a cry of dread at the sight of that burning skull.

"Who are you?" The thing's voice came without a movement of its crumbling jaws, rasping and scratching as if it had been dragged up from the depths of another world to touch the ears of the living. "Who are you?"

"Who are we? We are the friends and protectors of that girl!" declared Mustapha, edging his way to the front of their tiny band to face the grisly apparition. "By what right do you hold her here? Who are you, for that matter?"

"I?" The word shivered through the air. "I am Ahniz. My right was granted me in the beginning of time, my right and my sacred duty. I swore to them by my soul. I sealed the promise with my life. They killed the slaves, but no one dared to cut off the head of Ahniz! By the light of my brain I made this place. Other hands placed stone on stone, but the fires of my brain guided them. Men said my mother was Tsaretnaidos, goddess of wisdom. No human mind could conceive of such an edifice, they said. But no goddess aided me. It was my brain alone that saw the workings of each hidden passageway! My brain that doomed all profaners of the tomb to death! When all had been finished and the slaves were slain in the very passageways that they had built, the queen called for me."

"You mean Queen Nahrit?" said Mustapha.

"Nahrit the lovely, Nahrit the cruel," affirmed the floating voice. "She charged me with the secrets of her tomb, charged me to guard them in death as well as life. Death was my reward for having served her. No man would strike my head from my body, so she decreed that I be burned alive upon a pyre of spicewood. Like a phoenix I was to die! Not even the smallest bone of my body remained.

"Ahniz is a loyal servant. When the flames cast out my soul from my body, they could not prevent my brain from going forth as well to guide the wandering soul. I dwelt among the mazes I had designed, and waited. From this slave's body I took an arm, from that one a leg. Bone by bone and bit by bit I passed the ages in my craft, for I was born to build, to raise up monuments. Now I raised up a habitation for my brain and for my soul. Oh, mortals, this skull once wore a coronet! A greedy princeling wandered into my maze and died in search of treasure. This hand once grasped a golden sword! A faithless guard fell to his death in one of my pits, and I despoiled his body as I might take stone from a quarry for my work. I am Ahniz, architect to Queen Nahrit, and faithful even beyond the body's death!"

The green flames within the skull flared up fiercely at those final words. They rang in Mustapha's ears like the peal of iron bells.

"Ahniz!" cried Patience, taking her place beside Mustapha. "Ahniz, I was also once a servant of the queen. Her cruelty drives me from her service now. Let your soul find rest, royal architect. Do not waste eternity in protecting the one who slew you. Why do you hold the girl? Let her go and let us leave you in peace."

The green flames gazed at the peri and the hoarse voice seemed to muse as it considered Patience. "A peri," it said. "Well, let us speak with courtesy to her, at least. Daughter of Air, the girl is mine. Time eats away at all things, even the bones of heroes. Can you see the manacles that hold her? Bone, all pure bone that was not good enough to serve as bone of my body. I make many things from bone to pass the lonely ages. But my body too feels the touch of time. I must renew it. She trespassed my realm and she shall be my prisoner. The years shall wear her away as gently as the tides wear down a rock to sand; her bones shall become my bones, and her spirit shall be my bride."

The girl screamed at these words. She threw herself forward, straining at her bonds, but the rusty chains and bone manacles held firm. Patience strode forward, one hand upraised as if to strike the creature down. Her wings billowed out and seared the sickly glowing green shadows.

"Creature of unnatural life!" Patience intoned. "Release the girl and let us leave you to your silent halls. Release her, or prepare to fight." A thin flash of silver appeared in the peri's hand as she spoke, a sinuous ray of light that shaped itself into a slender sword.

The monster took a step back, cowering in the dirt at the peri's snowy feet. The clatter of its bony hands sounded like dice dancing in a gamester's throwing cup.

"Mercy," whispered the spirit of Ahniz. "Have pity upon me, and I shall show you wonders! I will help you flee Queen Nahrit, only do not harm me! I will even show you how you may evade the Hunters of the Queen." Ahniz groveled lower, skull and claws obscured by his tattered robe. His voice sank so low that Patience stooped forward to hear him.

"You must do . . ." mumbled Ahniz, the rest of his words lost in the folds of his cloak. Patience held her sword aside and inclined still closer.

"No! Trust him not!" shouted Elcoloq, springing back to human form. But his words did not come soon enough.

Bone clashed on bone as the crouching Ahniz suddenly leaped up and thrust a weird circular object full in the peri's face. Patience shrieked and fell at its touch. Mindless cackles of ghastly laughter poured from Ahniz as he stood triumphant above the peri's prone form. The thing with which he had defeated her lay pale upon her breast.

"Back!" warned Ahniz, seeing Mustapha and Elcoloq make a feint toward him. "Back, or I cast them both to their deaths!"

"Obey him," Patience said weakly. "He has not been idle in all these ages. With bones and strips of leather he has woven the sign of the seal, the seal that binds all peris more securely than any spell. I am helpless."

Mustapha peered at the strange object and wondered how a thing so small and insignificant might conquer so powerful a being as a peri. It seemed only a medallion of bone containing some kind of star in its design, but whether the star had five points or six he could not tell.

Elcoloq gnashed his teeth, forgetting how unimpressive his human teeth were in such a grimace. He would have attacked Ahniz, but Patience called to him and begged him with her eyes to hold back. Ahniz danced zanily around the peri, his bones clattering.

"You shall all stay here with me!" he exclaimed. "All of you! The peri shall serve me, and you shall leave your bones. Oh, I shall have enough to build my body over many times! And I shall try to build a second one, a companion more solid than the ghosts of these empty passageways. What can stand against the might of Ahniz? Not even death itself! Come, you," he called to Elcoloq. He picked up a second set of manacles and beckoned with them. "Come, you as well," he ordered Mustapha. "Put down your swords and accept your fate. I am Ahniz, who builds on the foundations of death, and you are mine."

Mustapha hesitated. He threw down the swords he carried to play for time, but Elcoloq walked obediently up to Ahniz and willingly placed his hands in the manacles. The monster chained him quickly beside the girl and called to Mustapha a second time.

"Do not resist me, mortal. The peri is mine. If you do not come willingly, I will command her to bring you."

"It is true, Mustapha," sighed Patience. "Who places the mystic seal on a peri may command her. I would have to obey."

"True, master," said Elcoloq from his bonds. "Even I surrendered, and you know what a fighter I am. Don't let him hurt you. We have no chance of escape now, not even the chance of a dog in a dungeon."

"I will not!" declared Mustapha. "Come and fetch me yourself, creature of evil! Come near, do not fear me! I have no sword. Ahniz the architect, were you? Ahniz the coward, you are! Let me see if those bones will break, you rattletrap phantom! I shall snap you in two like a bunch of rotten twigs. Your brain lived through the flames, but your manhood died, Ahniz the coward!"

His taunts were too much for the skeletal thing. The green fires sparkled with hellish light. With a chalky howl of rage Ahniz hurled himself upon Mustapha, swinging the iron chains above his head as he came.

They fell to the ground in a rattle of metal and bone. Mustapha had expected the skeleton to fall to pieces on impact. The bones held together and the creature roared with mirth, reading Mustapha's surprise.

"Ahniz builds well," it said, slashing at Mustapha with a heavy loop of chain.

Mustapha dodged the blow. The chain struck the ground beneath him, gouging out a thick clod of hardened earth. The man and the monster rolled over and over across the floor, Ahniz's bones digging deep into Mustapha's tender living flesh. Once Ahniz loosed the chain and hit Mustapha sharply across the upper arm. If the iron whip had landed any higher, it would have snapped Mustapha's neck.

Mustapha tried to keep his head as he wrestled with the nightmare. Ahniz's naked ribs stabbed at Mustapha's side like the teeth of a shark; his claws left awful gashes that ran red with blood. Mustapha fought a defensive fight, but his body was too vulnerable to the hard assaults of bone and chain. His defense began to slacken.

"Shall I tell you what you are thinking?" sneered Ahniz. "You are wondering how to kill me. Yes, how do you kill one who is already dead, mortal? There is no way! I grow weary of this game. I shall slay you now, and use your bones at my pleasure. All the riddles of death grow clear once you become what I am."

Mustapha's strength was gone. Ahniz tumbled him as easily as a lion shakes off a playful cub. Flat on his back,

Mustapha gazed up impotently into the smoldering green eye sockets. Ahniz raised the chain in both hands, ready to bring it down full on Mustapha's skull.

A bewildered cry broke from the monster's lipless mouth as the chain fell in a shower of white-hot metal. The white dog bounded into him then, surprising him and knocking him free of Mustapha's chest. Under the peri's watchful eye, the dog faded to a phantom and was replaced by the tall young man that Ahniz had so lately locked to the wall. The ghastly architect looked dumbly at the place where empty manacles swung loose beside the bound girl.

"Isn't that a shame?" said Elcoloq. "They fit my hands well enough, but my paws were a little too small. Ah, well!" He laughed and held before Ahniz's sight the ivory seal of power. "Forgive me, but I couldn't resist picking this up. The lady did not seem to mind." He slipped it into his pocket and laughed again, circling Ahniz like a trained fighter.

"You have not won," hissed the skeleton. "You may elude me, but you can never escape! You cannot kill me, and I will harry your every step. I will have one of your number at least for my use. Leave the girl with me and I will let you go."

"We do not deal with you," said Mustapha, joining Elcoloq as they trod a careful path around Ahniz.

"You will! You must! If I cannot stop you, I can harry you! I can delay you! Delay will be your death. Remember the Hunters of the Queen! You have not much time."

"Leave me!" cried the girl. "Leave me here and save yourselves! I would have died in any case. It is my fate. Please, please, save yourselves!"

Ahniz gave a contented laugh. His skull could show no expression, but he turned his head slightly to bow acknowledgment of the girl's words.

"Now!" shouted Mustapha, and he raced to join hands with Elcoloq, dragging the confused man-dog with him. Their linked hands formed a sweep that caught Ahniz across the waist and bore him almost off his feet.

"Ah!" cried Elcoloq, comprehension dawning. "The tavernkeeper's move, master!" In perfect timing, they joined their free hands under Ahniz's knees and continued to run with him. It was a move they had witnessed a hundred times in a hundred different taverns in their years of journeying, a never-failing maneuver used by the tavernkeeper and his brawniest friend to eject drunkards. On they ran, with Patience close behind, until they saw the gap in the maze wall through which they had first come. They stopped at the brink of the pit that had earlier trapped Elcoloq, and with a fine flourish they tossed their bony burden into the darksome depths.

Ahniz railed and raged at them, to no avail. Patience retraced her steps and returned with the girl, free of her manacles. They stepped gingerly around the perimeter of the pit and back into the passageway. Patience uttered a simple spell of closing and the gap in the alcove wall vanished.

"Do you think he will get out of the pit?" asked Elcoloq.

"Who knows?" replied Mustapha. "He may abandon those bones and build himself a new body, but that will take time and he will *not* use our bones. Now silence and speed."

As a child Mustapha had often heard the wandering storytellers quote the old saying "Evil has no memory." By this they meant that the worst soon passes and is easily forgotten. Mustapha now touched the truth of that saying when Patience came to a plain wooden door, opened it, and guided them out of the tomb of Queen Nahrit to stand upon the all-surrounding sands under the dusty blue of the desert evening sky.

They did not even look back at the tomb. The peri led them forward across the sands in silence. Elcoloq strode wearily on two legs and said nothing. Unused to marching any great distance as a man, he was soon the last in line of their singlefile party.

He suspected they were heading due north. There was a cooler scent on the seldom breeze, a scent of mountains beyond the horizon and green valleys nestled between. His paws longed to run on grass again. For too long all they had known was sand and stone, paved roadways and bleak wastes. Patience had given no indication of how long a journey they had ahead of them. Judging by the fairly small sack of provisions carried by the girl, Elcoloq guessed it could not be too far a trek.

When the tomb was out of sight behind them, Elcoloq ventured to whisper to Mustapha, "Master, what time do you think it is?"

Mustapha scanned the stars and replied, "Why do you ask? What use is time to us here?"

"Oh, I was just wondering," said Elcoloq nonchalantly. "I rather hoped to stop toward dawn and turn around to look back at the tomb. That was the agreed-on hour for the sacrifice to the evil one she serves. Now that there shall be no sacrifice, I would enjoy seeing if anything will happen—"

"You hoped to see his vengeance from this far off?" asked the incredulous Mustapha.

"Perhaps he shall cause her and her accursed tomb to be consumed by flames, or else will have them both burst asunder like a dying star. I only hoped—"

"Hope less for foolish things and walk. We will be far from that place before the dawn comes. It is hard to tell the time of night from this uncertain desert sky. It always looks the light color of morn or evening twilight. Walk on."

"I'm walking, I'm walking," snarled Elcoloq. They trudged on, stopping at last at a signal from Patience.

"I must stretch my wings," she said. "And I think you all could do with a rest. Take down the sack, girl."

The girl complied. She spread a fine cloth on the sands. Upon it she placed a quartet of blue and silver lacquered bowls and a series of lidded lacquerware containers, made bright with hunting scenes. Elcoloq laid down the cask of jewels he had taken from the tomb and fell to eating hungrily, with no great show of manners. Mustapha joined the feast in a more staid fashion. The girl and the peri shed their outer cloaks.

While Patience took a short exploratory flight to the north, Mustapha gazed upon the unveiled beauty of the girl. His food lay untouched before him. She ate as she did everything else, with the grace and daintiness of a queen. She became aware of Mustapha's earnest looks and met his eyes questioningly, a bunch of blue-black grapes halfway to her lips.

"I have seen your mistress and I have seen you," said Mustapha bluntly. "Many men would say you are alike in all your outward looks. They lie. You are the more beautiful of the two, for I have seen the difference of your heart."

The girl did not answer, but passed him a bowl of candied fruits. He took it from her hands and set it down. "Soon we shall come to Vair, that most lovely of lands," he continued. "There are many men in Vair who have palaces and great wealth; they could give you a royal house, where you alone should be mistress. Servants, jewels, splendid clothing they would lay at your most priceless feet. Music and feasts and dancing and revelry would be held in your honor. Yet never, Daughter of the Sun, could they give you what I do now offer, which is the heart of Mustapha. You cannot refuse it. It is yours, whether you take it or not. And if it should happen in the years to come, my lady, when you are the wife of the richest and most powerful lord in all of Vair, that you should see me with my trained dog entertaining at your table, give me but a look to say that you remember me and that will be my reward."

The girl dropped her eyes and said, "How can you love me? I am only a face to you. You do not know me at all."

"The sages tell us that we can read much in a human face," he answered, voice low. "They are wrong. The malicious and the wicked can hide their hearts behind a clever mask. Yet I know in my heart that no such mask ever lay upon your features. In the first moment that I saw you, I saw all the kindness and sweetness of your spirit, all the pains that had made you weep, all the hidden strength of mind that would not let you die under your awful burdens. How can it be impossible to love you by only seeing your face? It shows me your soul."

"If that is so," the girl said seriously, "then I cannot marry any of the lords of Vair, rich though they be. I have lived among riches that were not my own, and it was terrible. Teach me the tricks that you do to entertain the wealthy lords, Mustapha. Teach me, so that together we may make our way through the highways of the great world."

She placed her hands in his. Mustapha gave a cry of joy, hardly believing what he had heard. He almost feared to embrace his darling, dreading to awaken and find himself in a pile of straw in the castle courtyard of some northern nobleman. Elcoloq glanced up from his food and saw the change in his master.

"He is a great one to scorn my wishes," muttered Elcoloq. "All I asked was to turn and see the end of Queen Nahrit and all her evil. Ah, but we must all obey when it is some foolishness of his own forging! This is what men call love, and I have tasted it as well. Life was simpler when I was nothing but a dog. Love or no love, the pups are born the same."

Mustapha caught part of what Elcoloq was saying. "I was hasty, Elcoloq." He smiled. "When dawn approaches feel free to stop and see the fate of Queen Nahrit's realm."

"My thanks," said Elcoloq, well pleased. "It shall not be long now. Look yonder: Already the sun is rising." He pointed to the growing light.

Patience returned from her flight and lit beside Elcoloq. There was no joy on her face.

"We are betrayed!" she cried. "No sunrise could come from there. That way lies the south, and the tomb! She comes! Even now she comes! And before her, almost upon us—the Hunters! Flee! Flee while you can!"

As she spoke the light out of the south grew brighter, a burning, devouring light that seared away the very fabric of the sky. Darkness surrounded it; black clouds of smoke and ruin bore it forward upon their monstrous necks. Before the fiery light ran lesser lights, no less evil, no less sinister.

The lesser lights drew near. They had the shape of dogs—speckled dogs rather like a breed Mustapha had seen in northern lands. They were the Hunters of the Queen, and they were afire. Tongues of flame shot forth from the darker markings on their coats. They bayed destruction as if from a thousand throats. Behind them, supreme in the clouds of hellish brilliance, sat Queen Nahrit herself, riding down her prey.

"Take her and flee!" Mustapha commanded Patience. The sight of Queen Nahrit upon her infernal hunt had stricken him mute, but now he pushed the girl into the peri's arms and bade them go. His sword was in his hand and a look of slaughter was on his face.

Girl and peri hesitated.

"Do as he tells you!" Elcoloq barked, taking his own blade in hand and standing with his master. "We shall fight and we may die, but she shall lose her sacrifice!"

Bewildered, Patience took the girl in her arms and flew off into the north, never looking back. The two men stood alone upon the sands, awaiting the blazing tide.

Chapter XXI

TILL THE LAST
DOG IS HUNG

The desert was unnaturally silent. Mustapha and Elcoloq waited side by side in the vastness, hearing nothing but their own breath. The fire out of the south came on without a sound. Even the Hunters of the Queen had ceased to bay, as if already sure of the kill. Relentlessly they ran. The moon, slipping down the sky like a single tear, shone briefly on the toylike swords in the hands of the lone watchers.

"If I do not see you again, good Elcoloq," said Mustapha, "find a good master. I wish you a better one than I was."

"No such talk as that, master," Elcoloq returned, a wolfish grin on his human face. "We will be together—on this side of the grave or the other—but I shall not go over or under the earth without you. Besides, what must we fight and overcome here? Nothing but a woman and a paltry pack of hounds! May all my bones splinter in my teeth if I see more than three dogs running with the hag. We have defeated beasts of snow and beasts of bone; these are nothing more than curs. Ho, when I was a young dog, master, I would whip three times three such spotted mongrels for exercise before breakfast."

"I'll wager the dogs you fought had no flames leaping about them," Mustapha teased gently, eyes still fixed to the south.

"Ha! If you'd seen their size and the length of their teeth, you would not belittle me or make so much of these molten mongrels. The largest dog I ever fought would eat those three beasts for a snack and complain later of indigestion."

"The dogs that come run well," muttered Mustapha, testing his sword's edge against his thumb and setting his mouth grimly. He ignored Elcoloq's bragging.

Elcoloq noticed this, and it riled him. "That's it exactly. They run well. Part greyhound, no doubt, and therefore not good fighting dogs at all. It would be unfair for a prime dog like myself to dirty his snout with their blood. If I laid hold of them, then you would see how well they run, master! Aye, right back into the south they would run, and quick. Nyaah!" This last was in the direction of the Hunters, tongue out and thumb to nose tip.

"Rather than taunt them," Mustapha said tensely, "you might try to hold your sword as if you knew what you're doing. If you hold it that way you will drop it."

"Sword indeed! I need no sword to handle pariah mongrels!" Elcoloq exclaimed defiantly. He let the sword fall to the sand.

"Pick that up." Mustapha was stern. "You will not fight the Hunters of the Queen with your bare hands."

"With my bare hands? No, never! Use them yourself, master, and that sword besides!" The man was gone, vanished, and an angry white dog galloped growling across the sands, straining forward into the hot wind that swept before the Hunters of Queen Nahrit.

Mustapha was transfixed for a moment; then, when he fully realized what Elcoloq had done, he took off after the crazy beast, shouting and swinging his sword. But he was not fast enough to prevent Elcoloq from reaching the onrushing Hunters.

The first of the fiery ones was so surprised to see another dog hurtling straight for him, unafraid, that he skidded to a halt. The beast behind ran into him. Before they could untangle their flaming limbs, Elcoloq was upon them, biting and snapping and growling, teeth bared and vicious, seeking the best angle to tear his foes asunder.

The first dog was on his feet again but still confused, a wandering star on the desert. He lifted his head a moment to get his bearings. It was a moment long enough. Elcoloq lunged in and bit deep. He felt the hairs of his muzzle singe and frizzle in the flames of the other dog's throat, but he also felt his teeth meet, deep within that throat. Quickly he leaped away and the dog fell dead on the sand. His infernal fire lingered for a little while, then dimmed and went out.

Elcoloq had no time to enjoy his triumph. The second and third dogs were there, ready to kill. Nor was Queen Nahrit much farther away. With each minute her cloud of fire brought her closer.

The two remaining dogs began to circle Elcoloq, growling like ordinary market curs but burning like no beast on earth. Elcoloq did not turn to watch them, for he knew this old trick of fighting-dogs. Two or more circle, and when the dog in the middle is tired and dizzy from trying to keep both in sight, then they attack. So Elcoloq waited within the circle they made about him, hackles up, snarling and foaming but not moving an inch. The dogs began to waver. Finally the dog behind Elcoloq sprang at him.

Elcoloq heard the whispering, brushing, rushing sound of claws on sand and spun around to meet it. He felt sharply burning pain as flames shot up all around him, but he still carried the memory of real flesh beneath those flames—flesh he could tear. He bit and darted his muzzle into the very heart of the fire, seeking that flesh, and felt fire sear his mouth and tongue, smoke dull his eyes. Still he fought, seeing his enemy through the clouds of pain, and feverish with desire to kill the dog.

A bite, a snap, another bite, and again the sweet taste of the neck—the fragile, burning neck—between Elcoloq's teeth. As a fighting-dog, Elcoloq knew better than to waste time biting his foe in the shoulder or snout, but always sought the throat. The second dog went down.

Elcoloq was burned blacker than the shadows of the sand. Most of his fur was burned entirely away; his blistered mouth hurt so dreadfully that he could not close it. His tongue lolled out, beyond his control, and his feet would not bear him up more than a few steps. He tried to turn, faltered, then painfully forced his aching paws to drag him around to face his final enemy. The third dog, the fires of evil spouting from every part of him, waited.

Something about the third dog hinted at extreme age. Perhaps he had been the first creature made by Queen Nahrit's wicked magic. Perhaps he was a normal dog whom her dark arts had transformed. Perhaps he had also once spent years in some filthy street, learning the ways of a true fighting-dog. Something about him said that he was wise in the ways of battle. Now he continued to watch and wait.

Elcoloq realized that the dog was waiting for him to fall. The creature need not risk his life in combat, but had only to wait for Elcoloq to die. If Elcoloq would not die quickly enough, the infernal beast would leap upon him when he stumbled. If Elcoloq lost his feet, he would lose his life as well.

Elcoloq knew that he could not wait. If he must die, he would not let death come to him. Elcoloq gathered his strength inward and bounded forward with fangs gleaming, as if he thirsted for the very blood of death.

The third dog fell, its headless body toppling in one direction, the head rolling in another. Elcoloq stared through smarting eyes, confused. He thought he saw his master in the starlight, wiping a blazing sword against the sky to cleanse it. Mustapha has grown, he thought. His head brushes the topmost reaches of the stars. How fortunate I am to be the dog of such a royal master! We may have our quarrels, but after all . . . Elcoloq's eyes closed and he rolled over gratefully onto the cooling bosom of the darkened desert.

Mustapha could not believe what he saw. His sword was still dripping with the dark blood of the last Hunter, yet even as he watched, the shadowy stain upon the steel began to ebb away. On the sand the three prone dogs, their fires gone, also vanished, but the sand where they had lain looked darker, as if wet. Only Elcoloq lay still upon the sands.

Mustapha knelt and called gently to his friend, but the dog did not move. He saw the burns, the frizzled hair, the closed eyes. His heart denied it, but Mustapha knew what these signs must mean.

"You do ill to mourn a dog. You yourself shall die a more horrible death." It was a voice of cruelty refined by timeless dreaming, and it was *loud*. Mustapha looked up into the livid, leering face of Queen Nahrit, enthroned upon her couch of fire. She laughed and there were daggers in the sound; she smiled and showed beauty made horrible by years of ruthlessness. She sat in living fire, the golden scepter in her hand and the crown of tiger's-eye on her tawny hair.

"Stand, Sir Liar!" she commanded, and Mustapha obeyed. "So you are a diplomat sent by Ayree to me? Is this the way of proper messengers, to leave secretly when their work is left unfinished? You are no go-between for the warlock prince, but I shall make you my go-between. I shall fling you out beyond the bounds of earth, out into the famished darkness where the stars pour out their tears. There you shall wander for all eternity, never to return to walk among men until the last day is come and the last battle fought by your brethren. The men of garnet shall move before you shall return. Bid earth farewell, Sir Liar! Soon you shall see it no more." And Queen Nahrit raised high her golden scepter.

A torrent of silver light streamed down from the heavens. The stars of the desert wailed like living things. The ancient sands shivered and fled before that beam of argent light. The golden scepter glowed and throbbed, bathing Queen Nahrit with a wild, cold light until she laughed and wept and moaned with the pain of it, the power of it. Then the light subsided and she lowered the scepter. She stepped down from her cloud of fire and the cloud vanished. Scepter in hand, she faced Mustapha in the darkened desert.

"A touch of this and earth will never know you more," she said. "A touch of this scepter and even your memory will be seared away from all mortal things. A touch! A very little touch, no more than the kiss of a flower, and you will be hurled to the ever-mourning stars. Shall I touch you, Mustapha? Shall I send you forth to roam the trackless skies?"

"Your Majesty," Mustapha said hoarsely, his eyes upon the scepter as upon a snake, "I think you would find many men who would be glad to quit the earth. They would say you showed me great kindness in giving me such a painless death. The mercy of Queen Nahrit shall live in legend evermore."

"Fool!" shouted the queen. "Do you know the horrors, the dangers, the unspeakable emptiness that lies between the stars? Once only I turned my vision to look there; and saw things that not even I, Queen Nahrit, might look on untouched by the deepest trembling of the heart. There shall you go, unless—"

Mustapha said nothing, his eyes still on the scepter. The tip of that golden wand glowed and winked like a captive star of ice, like the eye of a silver bat.

"Unless," said Queen Nahrit, "you tell me where you have taken my slave, the girl." She waited.

"I have taken her nowhere," answered Mustapha.

"Do not lie to me a second time. Look to the south! That small cloud of many colors arising from my tomb is the flight of my loyal peris. Tell me where the girl is, or *they* shall be the ones to question you. You would not believe that creatures so beautiful could have a taste for blood, but I assure you, they do."

"Your Majesty, I believe it easily: Beauty is no guarantee of kindness, as all men know who have seen tigers or who have seen you."

"Be still! Tell me where the girl is!"

"I am not your slave, Your Majesty," said Mustapha. "Let the peris who serve you so loyally find her."

"They do not know where she is, nor can I get any satisfactory answer from them. I have no time to waste, so answer me now!"

"I answer no one who cannot control her own household staff. Wanderer and wastrel am I, but nobody's slave. Go and ask the peris for their advice. Better still, ask he that you serve with the blood of innocent women for his help. I know that he will be happy to enlighten you."

"You will say no more," said the queen. "My power is still strong. You will die for nothing. I will find the girl and Morgeld will have his sacrifice in spite of your petty heroics." She took a step forward, the golden scepter outstretched toward Mustapha.

And the scepter was gone from her hand. She cried aloud in rage and astonishment to see it held firm in Elcoloq's blackened jaws. The scepter turned, then touched her gently, like the kiss of a flower. A second time the icy light flowed through her body, but she did not exult or laugh in it. She screamed a scream of ages lost and dead, a scream of utter finality, a scream that trailed behind her like a comet's tail as she was lifted by the winds of heaven and swept away like the last leaf, the last petal, the final glory of a long-dead springtime. They watched until her form was lost against the stars that wailed and wept in the airless vaults of the dying sky. On the sands where she had stood lay the winking strand of the necklace that Mustapha had once given to her.

Elcoloq dropped the scepter, now no more than a golden

stick, to the sand and lay down beside it, as if to sleep. He seemed to smile once, in the way of his kind, then closed his weary eyes.

Mustapha softly brushed the few bits of Elcoloq's fur not consumed by fire. He murmured words of praise, words of endearment, secret names he had for his friend. The east was growing lighter as he knelt there stroking Elcoloq, calling to him.

"O Elcoloq, look southward," he said. "The dawn is coming, and you asked to see what might happen to the realm of the queen at that hour. See, the peris come toward us. Let them come. Open your eyes for a moment and see how gorgeous is their coming, like a flight of flowers."

The dog's eyes did not open. Tenderly Mustapha cradled the charred muzzle in his lap, not even reaching for his sword. A thin line of red lay glowing against the golden sands when Mustapha at last ceased to call Elcoloq's name. The whir of the peris' wings grew louder, thrilling in Mustapha's ears like a whirlwind.

A wall of sand like a golden wave rose up out of the south as he watched. It towered above the peris, and the outline of an infernal face was on it. The peris were dwarfed to the multicolored fragility of butterflies against that wall of destruction. Shards of jade, scarlet, gold, and silver twinkled woefully in that shifting dust, and Mustapha knew that he saw all that remained of Queen Nahrit's tomb.

The wave of sand curled over the swarm of peris and crashed down. Mustapha and Elcoloq were again alone on the endless desert.

He gathered the dog gently in his arms and looked to the north. A sister light of the dawn shone there, greeting the coming day. It was Patience, returning from the refuge where she had left the girl. Mustapha gazed off into the approaching glory of the peri's flight, then down at the small burden he carried. In silence he began to walk to meet the magic shining.

Chapter XXII

GIVE A DOG A BONE

The old storyteller folded his hands across his breast and inclined himself formally toward his young audience in the storyteller's traditional gesture to signify that the story was over. A reverent pause was followed by the sound of clinking gold coins that grew ever louder as the merchants and their children filled the blue brass bowl to overflowing. Some of the children were weeping, and a few of the fathers were trying to conceal their own tears.

The old man watched as the crowd broke up. The lights of Ishma had long since been lit, each stall illuminated by one or more merry little lanterns until the great bazaar looked very like the starlit heavens. The old man poured the contents of the bowl into a strong leather sack that he kept beneath his robes. He smiled as he felt the weight of the purse. As he set about rolling up the rug he sat on, he was joined by two visitors. A tall man came out of the shadows, leaning on a staff. He led a young boy by the hand.

"I saw the children," said the man. The lamplight gleamed warmly on the streaks of gray in his beard and on the silver bands that bound his staff. The boy beside him smiled at his father's words, for he knew the scolding would soon begin.

"They were impressed," boasted the storyteller. "Their fathers were also impressed." He tossed the moneybag high in the air, caught it, and jingled it near his ear.

"Impressed by falsehoods," the man said severely. "When will you ever tire of embroidering a tale that is impressive enough to begin with? Soon it will grow so great that no one will believe it. They shall think it was woven with warp of fantasy and woof of falsehood."

"They believe it," protested the old man.

"They believe it because they want to believe such things," retorted his accuser. "When they do not want to believe it anymore, they will tell their children that it is nothing but an old man's idle tale."

"They can say that of any story, even history. They will not believe in death until he comes to sup with them. And who knows? Perhaps they that do not believe in death will live forever! In any case, the children believe. That is the most important thing. You believe my tale, don't you, Beglash?" The old man smiled at the boy.

"Oh, yes!" answered Beglash, throwing his arms around the storyteller's neck. "I always believe you."

"My son," said the man with the grizzled beard, "you have heard him tell that tale twenty times. Each time he spins it out and twists it and changes it and moves bits of it here and there. You have heard twenty different tales!"

"I believe all of them," said the boy firmly, turning a serious face to his father. "I believe them because I love him and he does not lie to me."

"And do you think it right that he ended the tale so sadly and made the children weep?" asked the father.

"They might have wept anyway," the boy said judiciously. "It is better that they weep. If they laugh, they will recall the tale entirely as a joke. If they weep, they will not forget it so easily."

"Well, well"—the father laughed, leaning on his staff— "I see you have an ally, old friend. He loves you no less than I do. Let us go home."

The old storyteller gave the moneybag to the father and the rolled-up rug to the son, then stood up. He smiled, and the sight of that smile made both father and son laugh for joy.

"Who can argue with you?" said the father. "You are a rogue, and time will only add to the list of your crimes."

"Yet for all my offenses, you love me," said the story-teller.

"I love you well. Also I love my supper, so let us be gone. There is a good roast lamb for dinner tonight, and I shall not forgive you if we come home late to a cold meal."

"Never fear that!" said the old man. "I like my belly as well as you like yours."

"Nor," the man went on, "shall I forgive you if I hear you adding again to the number of the Hunters of Queen Nahrit. Last time you said there were two; this time there were three. Will you claim a hundred of them next?"

"No, not I," said the old man. "In truth, I could not conquer more than fifty of them, and that was when I was still young." The storyteller fell to his knees and vanished, and in the twilight of Ishma the boy Beglash, his father Mustapha, and the wise dog Elcoloq all turned their footsteps toward home.

"What do you find so fascinating in that scroll to keep you up through half a dozen nights?" asked Mustapha. "It is only a fable of the olden times."

"It is the *Tale of Oran*," replied Beglash, trimming the wick of his oil lamp and keeping his eyes on the yellowed parchment on the table in front of him. "I think it is more than just a tale."

"You have become a scholar," sighed his father. "You take no interest in the great happenings of the outer world. Your books and your scrolls are enough for you. Not even the rumors of war can touch you. The world will fall to pieces around you and you will stay here, like a mole, studying away in your burrow."

"War?" asked Beglash. "There are always wars."

"They say that this one shall be more than all the battles that raged before. The world is changing, and you lie buried in the dead past."

"The past is sometimes the mirror of the future," said Beglash, now called Beglash the Scribe for his great learning and his magnificent library. "There is something in this tale that speaks of such a war. Four swords——"

"Hopeless," sighed his father, paying no heed to Beglash's words. "He will always walk in dreams."